WATCH POINT

CECILIA TAN

RIPTIDE
PUBLISHING

Riptide Publishing
PO Box 1537
Burnsville, NC 28714
www.riptidepublishing.com

Watch Point

Cover art: L.C. Chase, lcchase.com/design.htm
Editor: Sarah Lyons
Layout: L.C. Chase, lcchase.com/design.htm

ISBN: 978-1-62649-674-3

First edition
November, 2017

Also available in ebook:
ISBN: 978-1-62649-670-5

WATCH POINT

CECILIA TAN

RIPTIDE
PUBLISHING

ABOUT OUR CHARITY

Twenty percent of the proceeds of this title will be donated to the Russian LGBT Network.

A Statement from the Russian LGBT Network

The Russian LGBT Network is an interregional social movement that unites various LGBTQI(+) initiatives across Russia. In the headquarters in St. Petersburg a team of 15 activists work every day to promote human rights, to fight inequality in Russia, and to build a strong and powerful community of LGBTQI(+) activists and their allies.

The Network provides various services to the community: we offer psychological and legal assistance to the people in need. Our Hotline services – land line and on-line chat – function 24 hours a day and provide assistance to LGBTQI(+) people in need across all 11 time zones in Russia.

The Network also provide Emergency assistance to the LGBTQI(+) people, who suffer persecution and prosecution, who find themselves in dangerous situations and fear for their lives and wellbeing.

In April, the world became aware of the fact that LGBT people in the Chechen Republic are being persecuted, unlawfully detained, tortured and killed. We, the team of the Russian LGBT Network, have been working hard to help these people to flee the republic, to restore their feeling of safety and security, and to find sanctuary outside of Russia. It has been especially hard since both Russian and Chechen authorities have continued to deny that this crime against humanity is happening in the North Caucasus. They need to hear our voices. They have to.

We are immensely honored that Riptide Publishing selected us as their Holiday Charity. Our philosophy is that human right defenders and the civil society are capable of ending LGBTQI(+) inequality all over the world. We, the team of the Russian LGBT Network thank you for showing you solidarity with the cause. Right now, we need you, because when we unite our efforts, we can create a better tomorrow.

With love and solidarity,
Russian LGBT Network.

If you are willing to submit a separate donation, please click the donation button on our webpage lgbtnet.org/en

You can also donate using our crowdfunding platforms:
help.lgbtnet.org/en
help.lgbtnet.org/chechnya-en

If you are an organization that is willing to submit a donation, please contact our Fundraising Officer at communications@lgbtnet.org

Follow us on Facebook: facebook.com/lgbtnet

For everyone who served our country,
even when our country didn't serve them.

The purpose of today's training is to defeat yesterday's understanding.
—Miyamoto Musashi

TABLE
OF CONTENTS

ONE

I used to think I was a good man. My mother died believing that I was. If I am, though, there's no way I should be here. I check the equipment: gag, restraints, hood, all in place.

Target acquired.

I knock on the door of room 212 at the Super 8 Motel three times: *rap-rap-rap*. Chase Milford opens the door without hesitation. Oh, sure, according to the app his name is "Randy Houle," but it's unmistakably him. He's making this way too easy. A gay hookup app, a secret rendezvous—he's already covered his tracks.

I stare into wide hazel eyes framed by blond-frosted hair, barely registering that he's already shirtless, wearing only running shorts. Never mind that it's December—apparently, this motel room is the Tropic of Chase. He licks his lips hungrily as his gaze travels down my body, then back up to my chest without meeting my eyes again.

I wonder what he sees. Hopefully only the superficial: cotton T-shirt a size too small molded to a hard chest, black jeans, gear bag and coat in my hand. At last his eyes flick up to take in my face. I match my photo on the app, black hair grown out, black goatee, a tanned face that could be almost anything: Native American, Italian, Puerto Rican, Hawaiian. I've been mistaken for all these things. (The last man who asked me "what" I was, was politely encouraged by a good friend of mine to choose between "American" or the slug of a .44 as an answer.)

Chase doesn't seem to recognize me. Good.

I push my way into the room, impatient to get this part of the operation over with, but I'm not expecting his hand to slide right into my jeans, his palm fitting perfectly against the bulk of my cock. He has mistaken my forcefulness for ardor and met it with unexpected boldness of his own. I would have pegged him for the passive type, a do-me queen. He's the spoiled son of a spoiled-rotten man. The last time I saw him, he was barely a teenager, a near-silent homeschooled wallflower. Maybe time—or a stint in culinary school, if my intel is correct—brought him out of his shell?

He's bold enough to cruise for gay sex via app, anyway.

I thrust into his warm hand while trying to make sure we move away from the door. It shuts behind me, and I reach back to throw the latch. If he tries to escape, that should slow him down.

Right now, escape seems the furthest thing from Chase's mind. My cock is hardening, lengthening in his grip, and he's making needy sounds in the back of his throat like the anticipation is killing him. My mind races. *You're here to kidnap him, not have sex with him.* A half-naked man is too conspicuous. I need him to put clothes *on*. I need to take control of this situation. I need to keep my head clear.

I need his mouth on the full package inside my briefs as he strips my jeans down to my thighs and sets his tongue against me. Fuckity fuck fuck fuck. I haven't been touched like this in forever.

"You hungry?" I hear myself say, and he nods, popping my boner free above the waistband and swallowing me. If I've ever had a more eager mouth, I literally can't remember.

He's on his knees and has worked his own hand inside his shorts, tugging on himself, and something in me snaps.

"Greedy little fuck." I grab him by the hair and pull him off me. "Who said you could touch yourself?"

He raises his hands like I'm pointing a pistol at his face, not my dick, but his eyes are bright and eager, and my blood pulses even harder. Eyes looking upward always seem beseeching, don't they? Those eyes give me ideas. "Put your hands behind your head."

He does it. I whip his cheeks with my cock, and he sticks out his tongue as if he can catch it, like a frog catching a fly. Ha.

"Will you fuck me?" he asks, and it doesn't come out wanton at all, just breathless and heartbreakingly simple. His need is so raw and undeniable as he adds "Please?" that I've said yes before I think it through.

I'm a man of my word. I keep my promises. If I don't have that, I have nothing. But I'm not sure promising to fuck my former boss's son counts as upholding my honor. I'm not sure of anything, because I can't think straight with all my blood in my dick instead of my damn brain.

"I don't have a lot of time," I add. I'm not even sure why. Maybe to remind myself that fucking him isn't my end goal. I've got to keep this operation moving.

"Okay," he says, like this is some kind of negotiation. "The only foreplay I need is, um . . ."

His boldness finally falters. He jerks his head toward the bed, where his own gear bag lies unzipped. I edge toward it, never turning my back to him, and reach into the bag.

Restraints. Rope. Leather. The heavy canvas of a straitjacket. Chains.

Chase Milford is a kinky fucker. And he's making it way, way too easy for me. "On the bed," I bark.

He scrambles up naked, leaving his shorts on the floor as if he moved so fast they fell on the spot like something dropped by Wile E. Coyote.

I know in that instant I *am* going to fuck him. I'm going to go through with it. It's just a slight change of plan. He asked, I promised, and if I need a justification, it'll only help me if I want to put him in restraints. Hell, it means I've already got his trust. Getting him into my truck might not even require a struggle. I'd like to avoid that. My beef is with his old man, not him.

Wrist cuffs attach his hands together, and I use rope to secure him to the headboard. If he notices the extra rope that ensures he can't free himself, he says nothing about it. His cock is red and straining upward against his belly, straight as an arrow, complete with triangle-shaped head. Pre-come drips from the slit onto the plane of his stomach, glistening in the bedside light. I used to crave that flavor, that salt and musk.

I have jittery momentary flashbacks to Cassidy, to Ruiz, to Garrett, three cocks I used to suck on a regular basis, on my knees in the back of a moving vehicle, rough cloth of their uniforms chafing my cheeks, a lifetime ago. I wonder vaguely where they are now, dead or alive.

The man under me is most definitely alive. I press my tongue against his cock and run it up the ridge, then tickle his slit with the tip and revel in the salty-sweet taste. His legs are free, but they twist ineffectually as he tries to push more of his flesh into my mouth. I pull up and work him with my hand.

"I don't want to come yet," he pleads, voice rough and breathy with desperation. "Please, please."

"Please what?"

"Fuck me first. Or during. Whatever. Please."

I had no idea Chase Milford had grown up to be such a slut. His father would shit himself if he knew. His father, Aiden, hates cocksuckers so much that he'll break a promise to one just for finding out that man is gay.

Maybe I should've let Aiden take that bullet himself. Maybe he would've survived it. Maybe.

There's no use regretting the past. I'm too caught up in the present: Chase is wiggling his ass enticingly, and I'm pouring lube into my hand and slicking him with it—cock, balls, hole, everywhere. I can't tell if the lube has some kind of stimulating chemical or if something about Chase himself is making everywhere our skin touches tingle. His noises have never stopped—like a puppy or a baby bird—something utterly helpless, utterly needy.

Getting the condom on proves tricky because my hands are so slippery I can't get the packet open. It takes bared teeth to do that, my need for him growing more feral by the moment, and I'm barely adequately sheathed before I search the trough between his cheeks with the head of my cock for the way in.

When I finally shove at the right angle—and pop, there goes what I fantasize is his cherry—his desperate noises stop, and he sighs like an alcoholic drinking from the altar wine, like it's everything that makes him whole, body and spirit.

I am suddenly no longer in a hurry. I am buried in a warm body, a willing man, a consenting partner. This part is true. He thinks this is what I came here for.

Maybe I did. That at least would be honest.

I begin a slow fucking the likes of which I've not often performed. Too many couplings in my life have been in haste, in barracks, on benches, all the more passionate for their brutal quickness. But there's no need to hurry now. Chase is at my mercy.

My cock luxuriates inside him, riding him slow and easy until his hole is fully stretched, then pulling all the way free to plunge in with sudden force. He gasps as if each penetration pushes the air right out of him, his eyes closed and mouth slack in rapture.

It's good. It's very, very good. When he begins to moan, there's a tinge of disbelief in the sound, as if he never dreamed it could be this good.

My hands are still slick from the lube, and I switch to short thrusts as I work his cock. He comes suddenly, far more quickly than I thought possible. Every muscle of his trembles as he turns to jelly on my prick, completely helpless under me. I take gouts of his come on two fingers and shovel them into his mouth. He eats it just as hungrily as he's taking my cock, and I come just as unexpectedly, triggered by something primal and deep about this coupling, something beyond understanding. I search his mouth with my tongue then, chasing that primal need myself, leaving us both gasping.

His eyes search mine for a few long moments. "You look familiar," he says.

Shit. "Everyone says that," I reply, and slump against him as if I'm exhausted, slowing my breathing purposefully, letting tension leave my body with each exhalation. He's caught up in it, too, unknowingly matching his breathing to mine as his eyes flutter shut. I'm lulling him to relax and keeping myself calm at the same time.

Before long he's asleep of his own accord, still tied to the bed, still covered in spunk and lube. I decide not to take any chances with him remembering me or getting suspicious. A little needle prick, a small dose of sedative—he'll remain asleep as I clean him up, dress him in some nondescript clothes I brought, and prepare him for transport. The operation hasn't gone at all as planned, but the outcome will be exactly as desired. I will have kidnapped Chase Milford without hurting him.

After all, I wouldn't want to lie in the ransom note when I say he's unharmed.

TWO

Time stamp: 0114 Tuesday, Natick, Massachusetts

My next stop after acquiring Chase is a rest area off the interstate that has free wi-fi. I park as close to the building as possible on the far side of the gas pumps, and a giant inflatable Santa looms from the roof over the truck. At this time of night, the restaurants are all closed except for one crappy drive-thru window, but even if the place is nearly deserted I don't dare go inside the building and get caught on camera. I can hop on the wi-fi from the truck. A wordy box pops up on my tablet screen, and I click on it: "I agree" not to commit any crimes through the service. I have a feeling if I get arrested for kidnapping, violating this Terms of Service agreement won't be high on the list of charges.

I send the ransom note through the darkweb. Anonymous. Untraceable. I'm demanding $4.17 million. It's a very specific amount, and even though giving a clue to who I am could be a tactical error, part of me is counting on Aiden knowing why this is happening. I want him to realize that if he'd just kept his promises to me, none of this would have ever happened.

Next stop is a mom-and-pop motel a couple of hours north of here, barely on the grid. They don't even take credit cards. I prepaid them in cash and have established a routine while staying there over the past few days. They think I get up early every morning to go ice fishing. The actual owners appear to be largely absentee and the clerks mostly underpaid local teens.

No one is awake at four in the morning to see me carry Chase into my room. He murmurs a few words as I lay him on the bed farther from the door. Starting to come around. I can't take chances. This might all be over within an hour. Maybe Big Daddy will get the message, wire the money, and I'll be on my way by dawn.

More likely Aiden won't even see it until after breakfast, though.

I've brought Chase's bag of gear with us because I left no trace behind, but as I look through his rope and restraints now, the temptation to use them is too great to pass up. I roll him onto his face and bind his wrists together.

He's murmuring something into the pillow.

"What's that?" I pull one shoulder back.

"Gotta piss." He hasn't opened his eyes. "Are we going to do it again?"

He still hasn't realized he's being kidnapped. "You wanna piss?"

"Yeah. Why, you into that or something?"

I don't answer other than to haul him to his feet and march him into the tiny bathroom. With his hands bound, I have to be the one to drag the cargo pants down.

He bends his knees. "Um. Aim me? I don't want to piss on your pants. It'll get everywhere if I just let fly."

He's right. And he doesn't seem put off by the fact he's wearing mostly my clothes now. I slip my hand around him and feel him quickening from my touch. "You better hurry up, or you'll be too hard to get it out."

"Working on it," he says, breathy, eyelids fluttering.

A hot stream starts to flow, and I can feel vibrations in my palm, the scent musky and thick, my own cock hardening like some kind of instinctual response. When he's done pissing, I shake him a couple of times, unable to resist flicking my thumbnail through the last drop at the slit, invading him just that little bit.

He wants more. His hips curl and he bites his lip. This one craves being violated. I can smell it in the sweat that breaks out all over him as I pull my hand away. I know his type. I *was* his type. I used to be the butchest butch bottom there was.

"I'm going to tie you to the bed," I say as I wash my hands in the sink.

"All right."

How a suspicious backstabber like Aiden Milford raised such a trusting son, I can't fathom. Chase follows me puppylike to the bed, leaving the pants and underwear behind, and my cock throbs. It's only been a few hours since I fucked him, and here I am wanting more already. This is the problem with sex, always has been. I do better when I do without it entirely. The need ebbs. But give me a taste and I'm all hunger. Not that I was different from the other guys on my team that way: once we got going, all of us could be insatiable.

Time to shut that right down, though. If the plan goes perfectly, I'll be a very rich man in a couple of hours, and I'll never see Chase Milford again.

I say nothing as I tie him faceup, limbs spread-eagled to the corners of the bed.

Then I sit back on the other bed, taking my time removing my boots. I can feel a chill coming from the badly insulated window. I check the latch, the blinds. This place is not the slightest bit soundproof. I dig through the rest of Chase's gear: sure enough, there's a gag. It's almost cute, a dinky black rubber penis that goes in the mouth like a pacifier. "You buy this online?"

"Yeah." He blushes deeply, though, like just being caught owning it is humiliating.

"You ever worn it before?"

He shakes his head this time.

I should resist. I should have better self-control than this. But a lot of virtues about me have been stripped away of late. I straddle him and rub the black rubber back and forth on his lips like I'm putting ChapStick on him. He whimpers.

"Is that your I-want-it whimper or your I-don't-want-it whimper?" I demand.

He closes his eyes. So ashamed.

"It's okay, Chase," I say, like I'm talking to a hurt dog. "It's okay to want it."

His eyes open then, full-on sultriness hitting me like Superman's heat vision, and he licks his lips. "Make me."

I get it. I really get it. He wants everything, all the dirtiest fantasies imaginable, but he can't bring himself to do them. But when the big, bad wolf comes along, it isn't Little Red Riding Hood's fault, right? Okay, Chase. I'll play bad guy for you. "Open."

"No." He likes being defiant.

Fine. This one's easy. I don't have to be physically rough on him to wrestle the gag into his mouth. All I should have to do is pinch his nose shut ...

But he's tricky. He breathes through his teeth, baring them at me, again daring me to force him.

There are other forms of coercion. "You'll take the gag now or you won't get my cock later," I say.

His mouth pops open like the beak on a new-hatched chick. Ha. I push the gag in, and he makes a satisfied grunt.

And yeah, I just promised him my cock later. We'll see if he still wants it when he finds out I'm ransoming him. My jeans feel two sizes too small.

I force myself to climb back onto the other bed, where I waste a little time unzipping my own gear bag and checking the equipment. I'm not carrying a gun. That's just asking for trouble in more ways than one. There's a fake in there that would be convincing to an amateur but not to anyone who knows firearms. The knives, though, those are real.

The most important thing in the bag is a paperback book. I settle back on the bed, turn on the reading light, and cross my ankles as I try to find the place where I left off.

Chase makes a whimpering sound. I'm assuming this is when he would normally make a sarcastic or seductive remark. But he's wearing this gag, see. *You're not really going to do the fake-nonchalant dom thing and pretend to read that book, are you?* I imagine him asking.

You bet I am, kid. You bet I am.

I read for an hour. He falls back to sleep, despite the gag, despite the ropes, despite his erection. Maybe it's the sedative still in his system. I check the time, then check my email. If a reply comes to the darkweb inbox, it'll set off a couple of scripts that will trigger a notification in the email accessible on my phone. It's getting harder and harder to be untraceable these days, but there are ways to do it.

Still no answer from his father, but he probably hasn't discovered Chase missing yet. I resolve to read for one more hour. If there's no reply by then, we'll move on to another location.

Reading is the only distraction I've found is worth a damn. Anything else I try, television, movies, music . . . my mind wanders, and all too often I don't like where it wanders. When I read, though, every sense is engaged, every nerve. My entire self is transported into someone else, and that's the best thing for my mental health, honestly.

When Mom was dying, I would read to her. She wanted me to read aloud because she couldn't hold the book anymore. And then we'd both escape into the world of Harry Potter or *The Girl with the Dragon Tattoo* or whatever her partner, Melinda, had brought her, saying their book club was reading it and Mom should catch up in case she got out of the hospital in time for the next meeting.

She never made it to book club, never left that hospital again, unless you count when she was transported through the pages of a book.

I realize I'm not reading, other than imagining what my name would look like tattooed on the inside of Chase Milford's thigh. His cock deflated earlier, but as I stare I see it's lengthening again, filling up and stiffening. His hips begin to undulate like he's dreaming about fucking, or being fucked, and his head thrashes a little as he moans into the gag.

Shit. It's like his cock and mine are connected. Every time he gets hard, mine Pavlovs right along. I free mine and stroke it for a moment of relief, but the need for more quickly surpasses what my own hand can satisfy.

I set the book down, move to his bedside, and loosen the ropes leading to one wrist restraint to give that hand a few inches of freedom. Not enough to untie himself or touch himself. Just to see what he'll do. To see if he'll do what I hope he will.

He does. He's not afraid to look me in the eye as that hand pats my thigh, feeling for my cock, finding it, stroking it.

So long since I've been touched. So long since I've spoken to anyone but doctors or lawyers or bank clerks or collection agents. The little voice trying to tell me this is wrong is silenced by how deeply right it feels in my gut. He makes a soft grunt into the gag like he likes what he feels in his fingers.

"You want it?" I hear myself saying. He nods enthusiastically. "Where, in your mouth?" Another nod. "Your ass?" Again. "Should I choke you with it until you can't breathe?" The most enthusiastic yet. "You're a sick little fuck, aren't you?"

This time he shakes his head no, though, and I can't tell if he's trying to show reluctance, trying to tell me to back off, or just disagreeing with my assessment of his mental state.

"Keep pulling on me. Nice and easy," I say. His hand hasn't stopped moving this entire time, and it's hypnotic watching the red bulb of my dick disappear and reappear from the tunnel of his fingers. Over and over. Pretty soon a big bead of pre-come has gathered, and just when I think it's going to fall he swipes his thumb over it, smearing the whole sensitive head, and I'm as close to coming in another man's hand as I've been in years.

Across the room, the phone in the pocket of my jacket vibrates. I can barely hear it over the harsh sounds of my breathing and the muffled moans Chase is making as I get close, but I do hear it. I force myself to pull free of his grip and check the messages.

There's a reply from Papa Bear. My heart rate, which is already racing from arousal, spikes higher and I feel light-headed. This is no time to have some kind of spell or episode, for fuck's sake. I force myself to take slow, even breaths. The text I just received has no content in it. It's just the last piece of a technological Rube Goldberg chain set off when my darkweb inbox receives a reply. Untraceable, but it means now I have to log in to see the message.

I take out the prepaid smartphone I plan to discard as soon as I no longer need it. Time for a quick access. I just need to open the anonymous browsing app. As soon as I remember the unlock code for the phone. That's hard to do with Chase making whining puppy noises at me. Impossible, even.

Fine. Is it really giving in to temptation when *he's* begging *me*? The gag is still in his mouth, but he's begging with every sound he can make, every motion of his hips, every bit of body language he can muster.

I pull the gag free, and he gulps air. "Tell me what you want," I demand.

"You want me to talk dirty? Is that it?"

I slap him sharply on the cheek—not hard enough to ring his bell, but to send a message. Obey or pay. "Tell me."

"I w-want your cock. I want it, all of it." He looks up at me as he talks, awkward and embarrassed at first, but his tongue loosens as he warms up, as his own words stoke his fire. "Want every inch, hard and fast, hard and slow, any way you'll give it to me, gore me with it, stuff me with it."

Pre-come is dripping from me now, and he's not even touching me. "Such a dirty mouth." I straddle his face and feed my cock to him until he gags. "You're sure this is what you want?"

I pull free to hear his answer. "Fuck me, sir, fuck me, please, anything you want, sir, anything."

Every time he says the word "sir," it's like a jolt of electricity zaps me right in the 'nads, making my cock stand on end. "Who taught you to say that word?" I breathe, sticking two fingers into his mouth just to make sure he doesn't go more than a couple of seconds without knowing he's mine to invade any time I want. I circle his lips with the wet tips. "You got some topman somewhere, some leatherdaddy gonna come looking for his boy?"

"No, sir, only you, sir. You're the only one." His eyes are glittering with a kind of triumph, or maybe it's just pure thrill. *Only you, sir.* Does he know how deep under my skin his words just went? Does he?

So deep I'm too impatient to untie him all the way. If there was any chance of me stopping short of fucking him again, it was gone the moment he said that. I pull a knife from the bag—not the really big one, just a sharp, useful one—cut his ankles and one wrist free, then turn him over and attach his free hand to the rope I left intact.

"Ass in the air. Come on. Up if you want any lube. Otherwise I'm fucking you dry." It's just tough talk and I know it—who would fuck without lube? He knows it, too, probably, but that doesn't stop it from being hot. He gets that ass in the air with alacrity. I waste no time in drilling him with a couple of fingers slicked from a bottle, corkscrewing until he groans. He's all moans and passion until he feels the chill of the lubricated condom between his cheeks and goes completely still. I'm so eager to fuck him that it hasn't even warmed up from my body heat by the time I'm trying to get my cock inside him.

In. I'm in. Now we're both still as statues. In the battle between my body and my brain, my brain takes this moment to force a pause in the action, maybe to force me to think about what I'm doing.

What am I doing? Besides giving us both what we desperately need? Right. I'm doing the only sensible thing. I'm maintaining my cover as a hot trick. I'm keeping him happy. I'm keeping him lulled into a sense of security.

I'm spanking his ass as I thrust, as he matches my rhythm back at me, meeting the blows of my palms and my prick. Sweet mother, it's so fucking good I can't think of anything else until after I come, until after I've cored him but good. I'm still inside him, afterpulses of my own orgasm rocketing through me as I reach around to give him a quick jerking off. It doesn't take long, the ring of my fingers around the head of his cock moving lightning fast until he makes a puddle on the bedspread. I flatten him into it then, biting the back of his neck and licking his sweat in a last indulgent overdose for my hormones.

Okay, enough. He's now either passed out, asleep, or pretending to be, and I tell myself it doesn't matter which. Time to get focused on the operation again. I pull the comforter over him to keep him warm and then check the messages. It's a bit of a process to get logged in and retrieve what I need, but it's only a matter of time before I'll see his father's reply. Aiden Milford made millions in pharmaceutical price speculation and healthcare consolidation, the kind of scum who'll close a hospital for not being profitable enough. Never mind that the job of a hospital isn't to make money, or that maybe it could be profitable if his own companies weren't also responsible for jacking up the price of drugs so much. I guess in his twisted mind that's win-win.

You can see why a guy like that needs a bodyguard. Rich as fuck and an obvious target for grudges.

The reply is pure Aiden. Arrogant, nonsensical, posturing, and stubborn.

TOUCH A HAIR ON HIS HEAD I WILL END YOU MOTHERFUCKER I HAVE NAVY SEALS ON MY PAYROLL NSA CIA FBI ALL IN MY POCKET WE WILL BE ON YOU LIKE A HEAT SEEKING MISSILE YOU LOWLIFE TRASH PUT MY BOY BACK IN HIS BED YOU STOLE HIM FROM AND ILL LET YOU LIVE

I have to chuckle sadly as I read it over again, making sure I've figured out where the punctuation was supposed to be. SEALs on your payroll, huh? A little out of date, that, unless he hired another after me. *I WILL END YOU?* The man has watched too many Hollywood action movies. The profanity and wording make me think he's sent this reply without telling his security team first. Pure reaction. I was hoping he'd get over that and formulate a more cold-blooded response. When Aiden turns cold and calculating, especially when it's about money, he can shut off his emotions entirely. I think when he does the calculation, he'll find that the ransom is actually pretty cheap and well worth paying. But he's not there yet. I need to give him time.

I have to wonder if the reason he hasn't told his own security about his son being missing is he's afraid they're in on it. Gotta wonder if he's screwed any of them over or broken his promises to them like he did to me. A paycheck is nice, but only loyalty can inspire loyalty.

Chase starts to snore. I'll let him sleep while I shower and get ready for our next move.

THREE

Time stamp: 0506 Tuesday, Pottstown, Maine

I brew us both coffee in the coffee maker and give him breakfast: nuked English muffin sandwiches I stashed here in the fridge. Time to get out of here. Another day pretending I'm going ice fishing, but this time with a friend. That's assuming anyone even sees or notices, which they probably won't.

Chase is still naked except for the restraints while we eat breakfast sitting on the bed. He asks casually as he licks his fingers, "Hey, so, where are we now?"

"You got somewhere you need to be?" I ask, just as casually. Or faux-casually.

He shakes his head. "Nope. If I had somewhere to be, I'd have something better to do than sneaking out for raunchy hookups."

"You worried about your car?" I wonder if there's a loose end.

There isn't. "I walked to a convenience store and took an Uber from there." He shrugs but his eyes are challenging me. *What now?* they seem to be asking. "My father would kill me if he knew what I was doing."

I can't help it. I lead him on. "He's a real hard-ass, huh?"

"The worst. Raging homophobe doesn't begin to cover it. I've seen him fire guys for even suspecting they're gay."

Huh. I wonder who besides me. I keep my face neutral and don't dare say anything.

Chase chuckles and sips his coffee from the paper cup. "The really rich thing is, I think he thinks he's protecting me. Like if I never get a whiff of gay hormones, I can't be tainted."

Ha. "Little late for that, isn't it?"

"Twenty-two years too late," he says, being truthful about his age. "Born this way."

When I was twenty-two, I'd already been in a war zone. "Me too," I say, but how I was born is nothing compared to the life that's shaped me. I continue to pretend I know nothing about him. "So you grew up sheltered."

"Yeah, you know, homeschooled, the whole nine yards. I convinced him to let me go to cooking school. He had a guy chauffeur me to class and wait there to take me back the second I was done."

"That's rough."

"Yeah. So's getting blown in the walk-in fridge."

Heh. I could picture it. "You're a hellion, aren't you."

He nods, giving me that coy, seductive look again. "'ts why I need a big, bad top to keep me in line."

The truth is I'm not that big. I'm more of a Bruce Lee than an Arnold Schwarzenegger—SEAL training puts lean muscle on, not bulk. But maybe he's talking about my dick. I wonder when we'll hear from his father next. "We could keep this thing going for a while longer," I say. "If you want."

He nods. "Promise me you'll torture your captive, too?" He gives me the puppy-dog eyes then.

"Torture isn't really my style," I say. "Unless you count orgasm denial as torture."

"Everything counts," he says. "Maybe a little light interrogation?"

"Like you'll be able to answer any questions with my cock in your mouth." I stand up and I notice his cock is doing the same. This kid is all hormones, I swear. I finish my coffee, crush the cup, and toss it into the garbage can. "You want to do this for real, give me the unlock code for your phone."

He spits out the numbers so fast I have to make him repeat them. "Good boy," I say as I dig his phone out of his bag. "Tell me which reward you want this morning, my come down your throat or your own."

"Yours, sir."

I want to tell him not to call me that. Call me Daddy or Master or whatever fucked-up thing you want. But I like the way "sir" revs my engine too much, too-too much. "Right answer, boy," I say, already unzipping. My cock smells like Canadian bacon, I swear. "Suck and swallow."

He's not quite as proficient at this blowjob thing as his bravado made him out to be. But since he's got the use of his hands right now, he fondles my balls.

I change the lock code on his phone, turn off all the geolocating services, and power it down before tossing it back onto the bed. Not a moment too soon. Maybe he's better at blowjobs than I thought. I'm far closer to coming than I expected to get while focused on the phone.

The orgasm makes my knees shake, and at first I'm not confident I'm going to stay upright.

But I do. He gags a little when he tries to swallow. Don't ask me why, but that's even better than if he'd guzzled it down like something from a porn video.

When he can talk again, he asks me, "Are you going to tie me up again?"

I nod. "Can't have you making trouble or running away," I say, looking through what other restraints and ropes are in his bag. It's a decent selection. "How'd you keep this stuff hidden from your father?"

"Stashed it in a shed in the woods behind our property."

I laugh. That's the kind of thing I'd do. "You're a regular Boy Scout."

"Never got to be a scout, so I just have to pretend."

I grip him by the hair and pull his face close to mine. "You like to pretend."

"My fantasies have always been better than reality," he says evenly, his eyes meeting mine as the tip of his tongue touches the corner of his lips.

My fantasies right now have put him in a starring role. What if he wasn't the Milford scion? What if I hadn't promised my mother I'd get revenge? What if I'd actually met him on the hookup app and this kinky joyride didn't have to end?

It doesn't have to end yet, that's for sure. I kiss him to see what his mouth tastes like after sucking me down. It tastes like lust and something fresh and new. "Clean up. I'm taking the restraints off so you can shower. But I'm going to watch you do it. I'm going to sit right on the toilet and watch your every move."

He grins. As if the real reason I'll be watching him is to see him suds up that lithe body. No, really, kid—it's just a side benefit.

He takes full advantage of the opportunity to show himself off, running slick hands all over his skin, sliding the motel soap between the globes of his ass like a credit card through a swiper. Good thing I just came, or I might be tempted to delay us even further.

When he's done cleaning up, I make sure he gets back into the clothes I gave him: cargo pants, a cotton tank top, and a flannel shirt. Not really warm enough for where we're going, but at least it's better than the running shorts he'd worn to seduce me. Thank goodness his coat's down-filled. His hands in front of him, I put him into police-issue handcuffs, telling him to keep his hands inside his sleeves because if anyone sees the cuffs, our little game could end really unpleasantly. A knit cap hides the blond highlights on the top of his head and darkens his aspect.

He grins conspiratorially at me. "Where we going again?"

"Ice fishing," I say. "You really wanted to be a Boy Scout? This is real Boy Scout stuff."

The place I'm taking him is a cabin that Garrett, Cassidy, and Ruiz set up some time before I joined their team, when they were convinced WWIII was on the way. A little hideaway open to anyone from our team. It's basically where you'd want to be if there was a zombie apocalypse and where we all agreed we'd meet if the government fell or UFOs invaded or whatever. Cass brought me here to work on the place when we weren't sure what was going to happen with our discharge. I've been back a few times in the past year or two, but I've never seen any sign of the others. Maybe once it seemed like the Zodiac was in a slightly different spot from where I left it. But maybe I didn't remember exactly.

We drive for another hour. I've tried to lay a bit of a zigzag route in case Milford or the police connect the dots somehow. That first rest stop to make it look like we were headed west, when actually we're going north. That sort of thing. I also overshoot the destination in order to fill up the tank with gas. Maybe they'll think we're on the way to the Canadian border, which isn't that far either.

Our actual destination is an island. One of the more than three thousand coastal islands in Maine. Before we can get there, though, we have to stash the truck in the storage shed, pick up some of the supplies there, and make sure the Zodiac is still seaworthy. I checked everything a few days ago, but isn't the Boy Scout motto "Be Prepared"?

The only thing I haven't been prepared for is Chase turning into as much of a lustpuppy as I was when I joined the SEALs.

FOUR

Time stamp: 0850 Tuesday, Pickerel Bay coastline

The sun is well up by the time we reach the shed. We haven't seen another vehicle or human since we left the interstate. This stretch of the Maine coast isn't even busy in the summer—what with a wetlands preserve between here and the nearest town, and the kind of rocky beach that's neither a good tourist attraction nor the kind of land millionaires want for beachfront property. In the winter it's utterly deserted.

I get both my pack and his gear bag onto my shoulders. After I lock the shed behind us, into the woods I go. Chase follows, his wrists still cuffed, his eyes wide with curiosity at the trees. The track down to the shoreline is overgrown a bit, but a fairly easy walk if one isn't hauling an outboard engine.

I'd debated whether I should inflate the Zodiac and prep it for use ahead of time or if I should wait until after I'd retrieved Chase. I'd ended up doing it in advance, but I'm still not sure that was the right choice as we reach the boat on the gravelly shore.

"Ice fishing?" he asks. They're the first words he's spoken in an hour, and there's a quaver in his voice.

"Okay, not really ice fishing," I say, piling our bags up. "That's a little more boring than what I have in mind."

I can hear the breath stutter in and out of his lungs, and it takes me a moment to register he's afraid. He's got his fingers twisted together like he's his own Chinese finger trap. Yeah, this looks like a setup because it is.

"I'm not a serial killer, if that's what you're worried about," I say. I take my gloves off. I've got the handcuff key on my key ring, and I hold it up where he can see it. "Give me your hands."

He holds them toward me, solemn, scared, but obedient. I hate thinking about what kind of father Aiden was to this kid.

He's not a kid anymore, I remind myself. He's older than I was when I enlisted. I take the cuffs off and stuff them into my jacket pocket. Then I put my palm against his cheek. His face feels cold. The winter air bites up here. "Listen. I know this is heavy duty. Beyond your usual Boy Scout shit." The words are harsh, but my voice comes out more tender than I expect. "Tell me if you can't handle it."

"Boy Scout shit," he echoes with a nervous smirk.

"Yeah," I say without elaborating. When I was his age, the dare would've been enough to push me to go along with it.

Maybe he's a little smarter than I was at his age. "This is something more than a hookup." My heart hammers a little harder; for a second, I think he's figured out I'm kidnapping him for real and he might be about to yell for help or run. But then he adds, "I mean, this is the first time a trick has . . . taken me wilderness boating, or whatever it is we're going to do."

"You turned a lot of tricks through that app?" The harshness I couldn't muster a minute ago suddenly grits my voice.

"Not too many," he admits. The air between us feels thick, like if I reached out to grab him, my hand would be moving through molasses. "And those that did, most of 'em were gone within an hour."

Does he feel the magnetic attraction, too, or is it just me? I cluck my tongue and try to lighten the mood. "After all the come you swallow, they at least owe you breakfast," I say. "I thought you were okay with a kidnapping scenario?"

"I was expecting you to hood me, tie me, and drive me around the block in the trunk," he says, wringing his fingers again.

"That'd have been fun, except that the trunk of a car isn't safe, and if we got stopped by the cops, there would've been way more trouble than either of us could ever want." I point across the water. Of Maine's thousands of coastal islands, some aren't even accessible to humans. Some are only to the very motivated. Garrett might be more paranoid than a bus full of meth addicts, but I send silent thanks to him.

From the shore, you'd never know that anyone had ever set foot on that rock. "No more driving around. That's where we're going. A private island where I can tie you to the bunk and fuck you next to a roaring fire." I sound so calm now I'm almost cold except for the emphasis that bursts out on the word "fuck." At first I think it's a mistake, like that's going to scare him worse. But then he steps close to me, runs his hand up and down my fly, and feels how hard I am. Throbbing. Just from the thought.

I try to play it cool, but he knows how much I'm burning for him. He still hasn't said anything. I don't know why, but the fact that he isn't a chatty airhead turns me on. I fill up the silence with more words of my own. "The hood idea isn't bad, but safety first, you know? We're getting on a boat. That's why your hands are free now."

He nods, and the look in his eye has turned sultry again. If he *had* been starting to worry I wanted something from him other than hot sex, his suspicion appears quashed by how stiff my cock is.

This is fucked up. I know it. But there's no going back.

"It would be nice to get away for a while," he says, and a thrill of victory goes through me.

"Can you swim? The truth, now." I feel like a hypocrite demanding honesty when the truth is that I'm starting to lose my grip on the big picture. The big plan. All I can think about is how much I want to get him to the cabin and bury myself in him.

"Yeah, I can swim," he says. "Although nobody would last long in water that cold."

Not even me. "I plan to stay out of it."

At the other end I'll probably get my boots wet, but there's nothing for it. The cabin's equipped.

"What do I need to know about this boat?"

"Mostly just keep your ass down," I say. This little Zodiac isn't like a military-grade CRRC, and I don't plan to hit top speed.

The sea's not too choppy. Which is good because Chase isn't dressed to withstand getting soaked by the spray. He's not even wearing gloves, for fuck's sake. It's a mild day for December, but it's a good twenty degrees colder here than it was when he set out from his father's mansion to meet me. The water's steel gray under the winter sky, and darker patches draw my eye as I steer the Zodiac away from the shore. Seaweed? No, schools of fish, clustering in the shallows.

We circle the island on the seaward side to the landing zone. It's near low tide, so there's a spot of beach that'll disappear in the next few hours. When I beach the Zodiac, I hop out and pull it until it's stuck on the rough sand. Chase joins me and helps me drag it a little further, but what's weightless on water is two-hundred-some pounds on land. I get our packs out of the stow bag, decouple the engine, and prep the boat to be stowed. Once it's in pieces, it's easy for the two of us working together to move it to a place above the scrub where it can't be seen and can't be reached by the high tide.

Only once does it seem like his hands are too cold, and he barely complains, just makes a dismayed noise as he clenches his fists against his chest after letting go of the frigid, wet rubber. I pull my gloves off again, and he obviously thinks I'm going to give them to him. I don't. I stuff them in my back pocket, take his hands in mine, and stick them under my shirt. His fingers are chilled to the bone as he presses them against my skin, steaming hot from exertion under my winter wear. My nipples harden against his palms, and he grins as he feels it.

"Better?" I ask as the temperature equalizes between his flesh and mine.

"Much better," he says.

"Good. Frostbite's no fun. We'll get warmed up once we're inside."

The hike to the interior of the island isn't too long, although there are a couple of steep cliffy places. Chase threads his arms through the straps on his gear bag to make it into an impromptu rucksack. Resourceful.

The cabin is as I left it a few days ago, stocked with food, a modicum of bottled water, and some other necessities. There's not a lot to see in a box-shaped cabin. The "tour" of the place takes maybe fifteen seconds of pointing at stuff: raised sleeping pallet, storage cabinets, weather radio. In the sixteenth second, the only thing stopping me from stripping him out of his clothes is the shred of common sense to get my boots dry. That means building a fire. A squat iron woodstove sits in one corner on a stone slab atop the raised wooden floor. I've already split wood, and I have cardboard and matches, all that, prepped from my visit last week.

A Navy SEAL taught me to build a fire, the first SEAL I'd seen since my father's funeral. I was a Boy Scout, on our troop's annual "survival weekend" in New Jersey. The instructors were two Army Rangers and a SEAL. They split us into squads and gave us various tests. One was to build a fire that would burn hot enough and high enough to burn through a string a few feet off the ground. Each squad was given only one match.

I hold the box of matches in my fingers, remembering.

"This is really nice," Chase says, still looking around at the place.

"What were you expecting?" I crouch in front of the stove and check that the paper and kindling are still neatly stacked.

"No idea. A dirt floor and a hole in the roof for the smoke, I guess." He shrugs.

"Some military buddies of mine built this place," I tell him. "We'd come work on it between deployments. If you don't build up off the ground, you end up with a lot of vermin and flooding problems, or so I'm told. If you really want to rough it, I can build us a shelter to sleep outside. It's a lot easier to keep warm overnight if there are two of you—"

"No, no, this is nice. I'm not knocking it." He sounds worried. "You've slept outside?"

"In a shelter I built myself? Yeah."

"In the military or something?"

"No, dude," I say with a laugh. "Told you. Boy Scouts." Okay, I decide I'm going to tell him about Boy Scout camp after all. "Two Army Rangers and a SEAL came to our camp and taught us stuff. The idea was if you were stuck in the wilderness with nothing but a Swiss Army knife, could you survive? They taught us to build a shelter, how to make it warm enough to survive in . . . if your clothes aren't wet." I get my boots and socks off as I'm saying this and lay them out on the slab. "And how to make a fire that won't burn out."

"How do you make a fire that won't burn out? That sounds dangerous."

Right. "Sorry, I mean that won't *blow* out while you're gradually dying of hypothermia. Like some serious Jack London shit."

He chuckles at that. "Oh man, I read those books. Alaska, right?"

Of course he's read them. Aiden has all the tough-guy classics in his library. *Robinson Crusoe, Moby Dick, Treasure Island. The Heart of Darkness.*

Yeah, whatever. "So, the test was to build the fire well enough that with one match you'd get something that would burn strong enough to burn clear through a string." One match. Here goes. I light one and the paper catches. The flame spreads quickly through the cardboard and ignites the dry wood with gratifying speed. *Ta-da.* "We were in squads of four. It was a competition to see who could burn through the string first. I had my squad collecting birch bark, kindling, bigger twigs, sticks, on up to small logs. You build a sort of teepee around the bark and kindling with the twigs and sticks, and then once those are going you gradually add on bigger and bigger sticks."

He peers into the open door of the stove. "Is that what you just did now?"

"Uh, in principle, yeah, but with the woodstove you just lay the kindling in one layer, the small split wood across it, and then the heavier pieces across that, and light it at the bottom." It's all caught nicely now. I gesture at him to get his own shoes and socks off. "Plus everything in here is bone dry, which makes it easy. The great thing about birch bark is it'll burn even if it's damp."

He lays his socks next to mine and then sits cross-legged, looking up at me. "Wow. Did your squad win?"

I'm not expecting that question. My jaw clenches. "No. Some jokers from a troop of older scouts just took their one match and—" I slam the door of the woodstove closed a bit harder than I mean to.

He gets to his feet in front of me, and now that we're both barefoot, it hits me that he's taller than me by a couple of inches. "And what?"

Might as well tell him. "And burned through the string. Didn't even try to build a fire." I had been ten at the time. Almost twenty years later and I'm still pissed off about it. "And the Rangers acted like it was all in fun." The Rangers did pretty much all the talking while the SEAL hung back, just watching. "They made a big joke out of the whole competition instead of disciplining the jokers."

His eyes are serious. "You don't like jokers."

"No."

"I don't either." He swallows, hesitating a moment before lowering himself to his knees. He does it without looking down, keeping his gaze locked with mine as he puts one knee on the floor and then the other. He settles back on his heels.

"Fire-building lesson over," I say. "Cock-sucking lesson starts now."

"Do I need a lesson, sir?"

There he goes with that "sir" business again, and my cock jumps in my shorts. This playacting thing really revs my engine. I'm playing with fire and I know it. "You might be my captive for a long time, you know. It'll be easier on you if you learn how I like it."

"Yes, sir."

"Hands behind your back. Or do I have to tie you?"

"No, sir," he says, then backtracks. "I mean, unless you think it's necessary."

"As long as you don't cheat," I say, "or joke around."

"No, sir."

Good, I almost say, *Good boy*, like he's a dog, but stop myself. "Now you're going to learn to undo my belt buckle with your teeth."

He doesn't need much prompting. The leather's not difficult to work and the buckle is smooth, no sharp edges to worry about. He gets it loose without too much trouble, but with plenty of rubbing his chin against my erection.

"Now, grab the corner of my fly above the button and pull to one side, then the other," I say, watching his saliva darken the denim as he gets the button loose. "Good. Use your nose to work the fly open, and get the zipper in your teeth." As he lowers it, my blood pumps and my voice vibrates with need for him. "Tha-a-a-a-at's it."

He doesn't need to be prompted to lick and suck my package right through my underwear, nor to pull the waistband down with his teeth and free my cock.

"Slow down, scout," I say. "This is supposed to be a lesson."

He nods mutely, licking his lips as he holds back from devouring me.

"Keep your hands back," I remind him. "Let me see the tip of your tongue. Now, with the tip, little licks, all around the crown."

He has to press his head against my stomach to get all the way around, blocking my view, but with every nerve ending I can feel what he's doing perfectly well. Pre-come is practically pouring out of me it's so arousing.

"Next, wet your lips, good and wet, and then suck right on the tip until you pull the head into your mouth—" I break off as he does it, before my words turn into obscenities. The sight of my cock disappearing into those reddened lips is as exciting as the sensation.

He intuits the next step, which is to pull back while still sucking gently, so that my cock emerges from his mouth but he never loses contact with it, and then suck it right back in. I swallow and try to get my words to start again. "That's it. Work the head. Just like that. Nice and slow."

Heavenly. I don't even have to move, just stand there with my bare feet planted against the wood floor, the fire roaring in the stove beside us, letting him do all the work. It takes concentration on his part to keep the suction right, not to go too hard or let go, and not to drag his teeth. He closes his eyes and gives himself to his task. That kind of care and determination would make him a success at whatever he wanted to apply himself to, I think, if only his father would let him do something with his life.

Now I want to test him again. "Okay, stop. Keep the head of my cock in your mouth. Don't move, don't flutter your tongue. Just keep it there."

I can see confusion flicker through his eyes as he tries to figure out if he's heard me right.

"That's it. Just hold it in your mouth. Yeah, I see you want to know why. Because I said so, that's why."

He gives the bare hint of a nod, but his eyebrows are still knit.

"You're my captive," I say, and the sheer wrongness of telling a lie that's the truth sends a thrill right through my gut into my cock. "I can do whatever I want to you. You're helpless and at my mercy."

Again that infinitesimal nod with his eyes.

"If I want to fuck you until you shit yourself and then make you clean it off my cock with your tongue, I will," I say, but I can't get it to sound the least bit convincing. Maybe it's the way my thumb is tracing the soft curve of his cheek while I talk that ruins my tough-guy effect. "But if you're good, I won't."

I can almost feel him vibrating with the need to say something. But he can't do it with my cock in the way. Is he trying to argue? Or say he'll be good? I suspect the latter, what with the way his eyes are wide and beseeching.

I don't give him the chance to answer, though. "So just keep your mouth right where it is. If I want to keep my cock in your mouth like a knife in a sheath, I will. For that matter if I want to sleep with it up your ass, I will."

My cock pulses with desire at my words, and he moans a little around it.

"You keep my cock happy, you keep me happy." I brush his hair back from his forehead with my fingers and stop talking. By now saliva will be starting to collect in his mouth. Another minute or two and he's going to have to either spit it out or swallow.

This is another one of those tests to see what he'll do. Retch, dribble, swallow, or something I can't predict? I see the alarm in his eyes start to build as he realizes it, too.

Some people aren't bothered by a mouthful of their own spit, but somehow once it goes past a certain amount, most people are grossed out. It starts to leak from one corner of his mouth, and his eyes get shiny as if the excess moisture is backing up into his eyeballs.

"What's wrong, boy?" I ask. "You swallowed my jizz this morning without any trouble."

A tiny whimper escapes his nose.

"Maybe I should add a little piss to it. Give it some flavor."

He swallows then with a grimace. "Good." Without warning I grip the back of his head, jam my cock down his throat, and hold it there. He isn't ready for it—which is the point—and he struggles instinctively, but I'm stronger and there's nothing he can really do but take it. His struggle is within himself more than a fight with me, as he comes to realize he's still breathing, not actually choking.

It's impressive to watch him make himself calm. Like something out of a Jet Li movie. The first time a top did that to me, I was far from calm: I fought until we both had black eyes, and then there was hell to pay.

"Good job, scout," I say. I pat him affectionately on the cheek. Then I slap him a little harder. "Enough now. We've got work to do while it's still light."

I'm only partly exaggerating. The sun sets at 1550 here now, which means we have tops nine hours of sunlight a day. He disengages from me and takes a huge breath. "What kind of work, sir?"

What the heck. "As soon as your shoes are dry, you're going to gather up kindling and starter wood. Next fire we build, you're going to do it."

FIVE

While we wait for his shoes to dry, I let Chase take a nap. After all, it was a busy night with not a lot of sleep. I change into my tactical hiking boots and split wood outside until my arms start to feel tired. I'm not in as good shape as I used to be. Then again, most guys are never in as good shape again as they were when they qualified to be a SEAL. The entrance test alone includes swimming five hundred yards in about ten minutes, about eighty sit-ups in two minutes, eighty push-ups in two minutes, and to top it all off, a one-and-a-half-mile run. The minimums are lower, but that's what you've got to do to be competitive.

I was very competitive.

When I go back into the cabin, he's awake. He's over by the woodstove, feeling the insides of his shoes. I see he's figured out about putting the iron kettle on top of the stove, and I can smell that he's discovered the instant coffee. An empty mug sits on the shelf next to the pallet.

"Okay, scout." I hand him my gloves, a piece of paper, and a small pouch. "Here's a compass. And the coordinates for where you'll find a birch stand."

He looks at the paper. I haven't explained how to read what's written there. This is another test, of course. It's not a test of whether he can decipher the military (and Boy Scout) map system. It's a test of whether he'll ask for help. How proud is he? How stubborn? How communicative? Is his ego bigger than his need to please?

It isn't. And even though I just had my balls emptied, it sends a deep thrum of pure want through me when he says, simply, "Teach me to read this? Sir?"

Took me a lot longer to learn to ask for help. I flip the paper over to show him the map of the island and explain how the numeric codes correspond to location. The beach, the cabin, where the Zodiac is hidden, and a couple of other points are listed in coordinates. It's not a long explanation, but it doesn't have to be.

Garrett and Ruiz had an epic argument over this map—over whether to create it at all—and Ruiz won.

Off Chase goes. I take the opportunity while he's out to check my contacts. Burner phone, accessing the darkweb.

The latest from Aiden. It's another rant.

COCKSUCKER I KNOW WHO YOU ARE
YOU WON'T BE SAFE ANYWHERE EVER AGAIN
I WILL FIND YOU I'VE GOT POWERFUL FRIENDS IN
WASHINGTON

Hahaha. Powerful friends in Washington. I bet they're useful when you want to fuck people over to make billions on healthcare. I bet they're not so useful when you're desperate to keep the secret that your adult son went out to have a gay hookup. By now Aiden's security has probably cracked Chase's accounts and discovered his last activity.

I've been counting on Aiden knowing who's doing this to him. Putting him through this much strife and worry, after all, is part of my goal. Even if it all goes to shit, even if I fail, get caught, or die, I will at least have served him a fraction of the pain I suffered. Wondering if someone you love is going to live or die.

It tastes sweet. Reading the panic in Aiden's words truly tastes sweet.

I send a reply and give an ultimatum. If the funds aren't transferred in forty-eight hours, I will no longer guarantee Chase's safety. I send a picture of a knife. It's a knife Aiden might recognize. I used to use it from time to time when he required me to.

My shoulder aches a bit from all the wood splitting, and I rub it beside the bullet scar. I need to get back in shape. I feel a little nauseous, suddenly.

We haven't eaten since breakfast. No good, soldier. I stow the phone away and break into the stores, contemplating what I'll do if Aiden decides to be stubborn and try to wait us out. We've got enough prepackaged food—MREs and canned stew—to last us a few weeks. If he gets more stubborn than that, maybe I'll have to teach my Boy Scout to hunt and fish.

Two cans of Dinty Moore—lids open, of course—are starting to warm up atop the stove when my scout comes in, flushed and exhilarated. "You've gotta see this! Something's in the water!"

"What is it?" I say, a jolt of adrenaline making me grab my jacket and propelling me toward the door.

"I don't know. Whales, I think."

Whales. So, probably not an approaching SWAT force. I grab the binoculars anyway and follow him to the promontory not far from the cabin. The island is under clouds, but where the sun is setting to the southwest of us the sky is clear, sending weak winter beams across the open ocean.

"There!" He points toward where the mouth of the bay narrows. From here it almost looks like the glistening backs of the whales are strange waves themselves, topped with wind-blown spray, but in the binoculars I can see clearly the spray is the blow and the occasional fin or tail. They must be immense if I'm judging the distance right. I hand the binoculars to him, and he takes a moment to figure out how to get himself pointed at the right spot. "What kind are they?"

"Aren't you the one who spent summers on Nantucket and whatever?" I rib him a little. "I don't know anything about whales."

He looks crushed for a second. Yeah, scout, it's true, I am not a walking encyclopedia about everything and anything. Whale species are outside my expertise. Ask me all you want about weapons, though.

He looks at them again. "I think they're either humpbacks or finbacks," he says then. "One of the big types, anyway. Can't tell with how far away they are."

Even with my bare eyes, I can see it when one jumps out of the water. Then several large heads all emerge at once.

"They must be feeding," he says.

"Yeah. If they were just migrating, they would've passed out of sight by now."

"I thought you didn't know anything about whales?" he jokes.

"'Anything' is a relative term," I say. My voice sounds remarkably unjaded. "I used to see them from ships all the time."

He nods and raises the binoculars. "They might not be migrating, but maybe the fish are. If a large school is trying to get in or out of the bay, they get concentrated by the outcropping and *bam*, all-you-can-eat buffet. If you're a whale, anyway."

We lapse into silence and watch the whales. Well, Chase watches the whales and I find myself watching him. I'm entranced by the wind ruffling his hair. He's oblivious to the deepening cold, entranced by the dance of nature in front of him. It's true I've seen whales plenty of times before, from ships, from helicopters, from drop planes. But somehow standing here beside him, it's like I'm seeing them for the first time, through Chase's eyes.

The sun dips below the horizon all too soon. "Come on," I say. "Dinner's waiting, and I still haven't fucked you by the fire like I promised."

He grins. "Sounds good."

Back at the cabin we hang up our outerwear and shuck our footwear. I stoke the fire, then go looking for the spoons. Takes me a couple of minutes to find them. I use my work gloves like pot holders and transfer the two cans of stew to the rough table, a spoon sticking out of each.

He's adding something to the map, using his fingers to measure the grid and placing a point. On the flip side, he adds to the list of coordinates. Below "Latrine" and above "Well" he writes in "Watch Point."

I pour us both bottled water. He digs into his stew hungrily, burns his tongue, then grins at me. "Well, that was worth the trip to an island at the edge of nowhere."

I stir my stew. I'm balanced on the stool, the balls of my feet on the floor, one heel going like a small sewing machine. "And here I thought you came here for my cock."

"No, sir," he says with a gleam of mischief. "You brought me here to service your cock. There's a difference."

"Hm, true." I take a careful bite, savoring beef and gravy. "Do you want to play it that way? Sometimes? The whole unwilling captive thing, I mean."

"We could play it that way," he says. "It's hot as fuck, after all."

I nod. *Hot as fuck* is an understatement. My jeans are getting tight just thinking about it. "We'd have to be careful, though. Not to really injure each other. There's no walk-in ER around here." To put it mildly.

He licks his lips, and it's not because the stew is salty. "I don't really know how to fight anyway."

"You can hurt someone even pretending to fight," I say. "How's this for a rule. If we're going to do this whole against-your-will thing, you can fight, but no weapons, no objects. And you have to give up once I get my cock in you."

"That's reasonable." He's now staring at his stew like he's too excited to eat it.

"Eat," I say. "You're going to need your strength if we're going to play it like that."

"Okay."

We eat in silence a while, each in our own thoughts. I can't stop watching him, though, the way his mouth moves, his cheeks slightly reddened from windburn and his hair a mess. He's more beautiful like this—rough from the outdoors and wearing one of my flannel shirts—than he was when freshly groomed and dressed for a trick. I'm watching him so closely I see the moment a wistful expression crosses his eyes.

"What are you thinking?" I ask, to see if he'll tell me.

He gives a little shrug, examining the table. "I feel like I'm asking a lot."

"Eyes up," I say, and he looks at me. "Ask for what you want. If we're going to be—" I veer away from the word *lovers* at the last second and instead use the word "—intimate." It doesn't sound any better. "If we're *going to fuck*, I want honesty." The irony only burns a little in my throat.

He swallows, though, still afraid to ask something. "I don't want to come across as pushy."

Oh, so that's what it is. "Don't worry, scout. If I think you're too pushy, I'll just put you in your place."

"Oh." A kind of relief settles over him. I wonder who in his past quit loving him for asking for what he wanted. "It's just . . . Okay. It's mainly that the Boy Scout stuff today was cool, too, you know? I don't want to . . . to lose that, either. But I probably have to choose between that or going all-in on this captive thing, right?"

He's so prepared to be disappointed. I can see it in the cant of his shoulders, the half cringe in his eyes, like a dog expecting to be swatted. "Not everything in life has to be a trade-off," I say. "How about this? Boy Scout by day, captive by night."

His eyes light up and he sits taller, like the burden on his shoulders has been lifted. "That's . . . a great idea."

"Yeah. I'm glad I thought of it." I scrape the last of the stew out of my can and wash it down with a swig of water from the bottle. "You done eating?"

He nods, suddenly alert and unsure if we're starting already.

We are. I stand up. I strip out of my shirts, down to bare skin. The cabin's quite warm now that the stove's been burning steadily for a couple of hours. His eyes rove over my bare chest and arms. "I captured you for one reason and one reason only," I say. "To serve my cock. To make you my sex slave."

He takes one last nervous drink of water, and then gets up himself and backs away from me. "Y-you can't do that."

"There's no one here to help you. No way out. You want to run? Try it." I rub my hand up and down the bulge in my jeans, and it feels like I'm cocking the hammer of a gun. "Your toes will freeze off before you even reach the water, and the rest of you will follow if you try to swim for it."

He gives up on dialogue, just makes a kind of dismayed shout and lunges for the door.

I have him trapped against it before he can unbar it. My erection is pressed right between his cheeks, and I'm wishing for some magic way to make our clothes disappear. I'd fuck him right here, like this, if I could.

I put him into an only half-effectual headlock, but he's playing along enough that he doesn't escape from it. I manage to get his cargo pants and underwear down to the middle of his thighs. When I try to wrap my fingers around his cock, though, he twists away. He tries to run, but his pants have dropped around his knees and he almost falls.

I tackle him onto the sleeping pallet, where the sleeping bag from his nap earlier is still spread across the insulating pad. I pin him facedown. He's trying to struggle as I kick his pants off with one of my own feet and then, with one of my knees in his back, I get my belt open. This gives me an idea. I slip it free and loop it around his neck by holding the ends together close to his spine. It's not looped through the buckle—if I let go, it'll fall right off—but it must feel like a noose to him. He goes still, panting. Now that I've got ahold of him, I can use my other hand to dig the tube of lube out of the gear bag next to the bed.

I toss it down in front of him. "Your choice. You can lube yourself up nice and good, or you can take your chances."

I can't help but grin when he chooses to try to escape one more time, gripping the edges of the belt with his fingers and thrashing back and forth. While he struggles, I grit my teeth and growl in his ear, "You know the Boy Scout motto's 'Be Prepared,' right? Before sundown tomorrow it'll be your job to lube up. Because I might not be so nice next time."

He gives me that little nod of "yes" even as he's trying to get free. He doesn't succeed. I cut off his oxygen just enough that he has to give up the fight. To reward him when he goes still again, I let him breathe. "Put some lube in my hand. Come on. Do it."

He uncaps it and squirts a dollop into my open palm. I slick my cock with it, groaning. I can't believe how hard I am. I swear my dick feels bigger in my hand than usual.

By unspoken agreement he doesn't struggle while I sheathe myself in a tight condom, but once I get one slick finger into him, he starts struggling again. I let go the belt this time and use both hands to wrestle him, trying to get my cock into him. It's hot as hell but much more difficult to do than I expected. The fight is foreplay for every part of me, though, mind and body, every muscle, every nerve, every sense fully engaged in this one goal: penetrate him.

I'm not sure if it's that he tires before I do or if he starts subtly cooperating, but his core muscles stop straining so much and his struggles reduce to his arms flailing and reaching for purchase. That's the break I need to get the angle right and jam my cock into him.

He screams and the sound alone almost makes me come. Sweet mother of God, what a sound, primal and raw. It's everything. My entire body is throbbing like my cock, my ears ringing, my lungs pumping, my forearms straining to hold us in this position. Sublime. Time stops except for the hammering of my heart.

He's clenched so tight I'm not even all the way in. "This is what I brought you here for, boy," I say. There I go again, trying to give it a gangster growl, but it comes out breathless.

He whimpers and pushes invisibly back against me. "My daddy always warned me not to talk to strangers," he says. "Always said my ass was what they wanted. Always said some big, bad man would rape me if I wasn't good."

Goose bumps spread across my back like a sudden sleet storm. He's playacting, but I can't help but imagine Aiden saying something like that.

Time to playact back at him. "Is it your first time, boy?"

"Yes, sir." He heaves a dry sob. "I'm a virgin!" His next sob is a little too close to a laugh, though.

Trying to keep things serious, I tamp down the urge to snicker. "Not anymore," I say, and give a brutal snap of my hips. "This sweet ass is mine."

"Daddy was right!"

"Yeah, kid, Big Daddy was right." I pull back and slam forward again. "He knew cock was your future." Another slam. "He just didn't want to admit it."

The next sob sounds more real, and I wonder if that was way too close to the truth. I resolve to shut up for a while and enjoy the ride. Chase fills the gap left by my silence with protests and begging. "No, please! Stop! Oh God." Nonstop.

It's far hotter than I imagined it would be. I don't think I've ever fucked so hard or come so hard in my life. When I strip the condom off, my cock is coated in slime and still insanely hard. I flip him over and rut against him, rubbing my cock against his as it slowly softens, stroking both of us in my hand. After I go soft, I add a dollop of lube to my palm and stroke him.

"That's it," I hear myself saying. "Here's a little taste of what to expect on my watch. When you're good, sometimes I'll let you come. When you're not, well, all I want is that hole of yours."

His groan is pure lust, any pretense of protest overwhelmed by the needs of the thrusting organ in my fingers. His face is as red as his cock as he pants with effort. My hand slows from a blur to a long, firm stroke, his hips rising to meet me, and suddenly I'm pumping a squirt of jizz on each stroke.

He collapses with a tired noise. I want nothing more than to lie down next to him and pass out for an hour or two, but there's the fake captor role to maintain.

And the real captor role, too. I realize this arrangement is going to work to my advantage in the best possible way. Not only can I fuck Chase Milford as often as I want, but he's not going to object if I lock him up for the night so I can get some sleep.

The only drawback to this unwilling captive thing is that now I have to be the one to fetch the water to clean us up. I handcuff him to the bedpost, but I'm already making a mental list of tasks to have the scout do tomorrow before sundown.

SIX

Time stamp: 0721 Wednesday, Ledge Island

I open my eyes and am startled to see sunlight coming through the high windows. They were another Garrett feature, all of them installed seven feet up—crank-style windows, a few feet wide but only eight inches tall. They let in light and let out heat in the summer, but they're defensible and if one were to get broken by, say, flying debris in a windstorm while the cabin's unoccupied, the hole would still keep out most of the rain and wild animals.

How did it get to be daylight already? Did I really sleep almost twelve hours? I haven't slept that well or long in years. I expect my body to feel like lead, but I feel light, like the bed platform is a raft, floating on water.

I move slowly while I attempt to determine if Chase is awake. If he is, he's feigning sleep, curled on his side away from me, still wearing the metal handcuffs, looped by a chain around the bedpost.

One of his hands is shaking, though. Trembling. And I can see his fingernails look a little blue.

Shit! What seemed like a sexy idea last night, hiding the handcuff key in my underwear, seems *stupid, stupid, stupid* now as I peel the key off my balls. I wake him up with my hurried unlocking of the cuffs and the cursing under my breath.

"What's wrong?" he asks sleepily.

The cuffs hit the wooden floor with a *thud* and I've got his hand between mine. It feels cold, cold. *Stupid, stupid, stupid.* This is just the kind of miscalculation I can't afford. All because I'm using my dick instead of my brain. My voice comes out morning rough, barely audible. "Please be okay."

"I'm fine, what—" He's starting to clue in that something's wrong, though. As circulation returns to his hand, the pins and needles start. "Ow, ow, ow!"

He tries to pull out of my grip, as if I'm what's causing the pain. Who am I kidding? I did cause it. Just not directly. "Hold still."

Something in my chest does a flip when he instantly obeys me. I reward him with an explanation. "You got twisted in the cuffs while you slept. The hard edge of the metal cut off the circulation to your hand."

"Oh." He grimaces as the pins and needles must be getting worse.

"If it hurts, that's a good sign," I say.

"It feels hot." He wiggles his fingers in my grip. "It still works."

"Let me look at it." I let go and cradle his hand in my lap. Color's getting back to normal, but it still feels cold. He wiggles his fingers again, and this time my bark is sharp. "I said *hold still!*"

He blanches. "I-I'm sorry."

I'm too busy examining his hand and fingers to notice his face at first. When I finally look directly at him, I see he's stifling tears. When he sees I've "caught" him having this emotion, an apology spills out again. "I won't do it again. Please don't be mad at me."

What? I blink, trying to understand. "I'm not mad at you," I say. "I'm mad at myself."

"Oh." He doesn't seem to comprehend what I've said any better than I comprehend him.

"I shouldn't have let you spend the whole night in handcuffs." I get to my feet, trying not to sound angry, but I'm still blaming myself hard. *There are safer ways to do that, you stupid fuck. You got lazy. Don't let it happen again.* I remind myself it's Scout time now. Lesson learned. "You tell me if you feel tingling or anything with that hand or your fingers, okay?"

"Okay." He's sitting up cross-legged on the pallet now, flexing his fingers, but his eyes are on me. He's tamping down his emotions like a good little soldier. "Okay. What are we learning today, sir?"

"We are learning that losing precious daylight to sleep is a one-time thing." I start heating the kettle. "You wanted to learn to build a shelter? We'll build a shelter."

"You mean that?"

I nod slowly. "Did you think I was kidding?"

"I dunno. Sometimes people say things they don't really mean." He's got a gleam of challenge in his eye, and I wonder who he thinks he's standing up to. Oh, who am I kidding. There's no way he grew up with Aiden for a father without massive daddy issues.

I feel like a heel, but it has to be said: "I try not to. Now come on. Breakfast first. Then we've got branches to cut." And while we're at it, I think, we can cut some branches for putting on the roof and eaves of the cabin to soften the outline and camouflage it from prying eyes. You can't even see the cabin from a boat on the water—the promontory blocks the view from the ocean side and the trees block it from the shore side—but you could from a helicopter.

Not that I think it'll come to that. But there's no reason not to prepare for every possibility.

"Okay, let's pretend we got stranded on this island and it could be days until we're rescued." I've led him to a copse of trees that's evergreens on the northern side, deciduous on the southern side, and a mix in the middle. "So we need shelter. Where do you think would be the best place to do that?"

He's got his hands deep in his coat pockets as he looks around. "I bet we want somewhere dry."

"Good. The number one thing that could kill us is the cold, and the way the cold gets you is through you being wet or damp. If it's below sixty-five degrees and you can't get dry, you're dead in three days."

"Sixty-five doesn't sound that cold." He stamps his feet, no doubt feeling that it's half that temperature here right now.

"I know, but it's thirty degrees colder than your body temperature, and five degrees colder than the temperature at which the body dies. If your clothes are wet, you're leaching that heat away constantly." I shrug to indicate the finality of the problem. "Hypothermia's a bitch, too, because it fucks with your mind. As your body tries to conserve heat in your core, your brain is one of the parts that gets shorted. Confusion, amnesia, insanity. It can all happen from your body temperature getting too low."

"Wow."

"It can happen slowly if you're damp, or fast, if you fall into cold enough water." We almost lost a man once on a training mission in Alaska. After we pulled him out of the water he kept trying to fight us off, convinced we were trying to kill him instead of help him. Cold can make you nuts. I decide not to tell Chase that story right now. "Anyway. What looks the driest?"

He takes a walk around a tall pine with no branches until near its crown. "Hm. Well, between the trees the ground's the highest, but the overhead cover's the thinnest and it might rain. So, I don't know."

"Good thinking, but generally it'll be drier under the trees as long as the tree isn't in a dip in the ground. Let's look for two trees close together that are on a bit of a rise." I can see a good spot, but I'm determined to let him choose where we do this. "About two meters apart. But not too rooty or it won't be very comfortable to sleep on."

He walks among the trees for a bit, then asks, "Is it better to be on pine needles or regular leaves?"

"Either one could be good, but you'll see," I say.

"And should they be skinny trees?"

"Yeah, but you'll find if two trees are going to be that close together, they're usually pretty skinny."

"Gotcha." He finds a nice pair of aspens. "Two meters is around six feet, right? Are these birch? You said birch was good for building fires."

"Yes, I did. These are aspen, but close enough." I point to the ground between them. "First thing: check out the ground between them. No ant nests or animal burrows, no big rocks sticking up, no wet areas."

The area is leaf-covered, of course. He begins picking through the leaves with his hands. He's wearing my work gloves and I cringe a little. "It's kind of damp underneath."

"It's always going to be a little damp under ground litter like that. Why don't you pick up that branch and use it like a broom?" I point to a branch on the ground that must've come down recently. It's still got some leaves on the end.

He sweeps clear the patch between the trunks. Looks good. The ground is firm. "In an emergency, like if we landed here with only an hour until dark and had to move fast, I'd look for a fallen tree that makes a kind of natural tent. But the problem with a natural shelter is you might not be the only animal wanting to shelter there."

"And we've got all day."

I chuckle. "Yeah, all seven hours of it we have left. Let's assume we've got a rope and a knife to work with, but nothing else."

"Okay. What's next?"

"If we had a tarp we could make a kind of tent, but let's pretend we don't even have that. Let's build a lean-to. Next step: tie a crossbar between the two trunks. Go find a fallen branch that's long enough and sturdy enough, but not too thick."

He hares off into the woods before I can tell him not to go too far or he'll end up having to drag it a long way. I hear him circling around, though, whistling to himself. The island's got no bears and the area doesn't even have poisonous snakes, so I'm not too worried. The way he's crashing around, anything that might bite him is well scared off, anyway.

He comes back dragging a small sapling, nice and straight and branchless until the top. He's a little out of breath as he drops his find in front of me. "Check this one out! It was broken off where a spruce fell over there."

"How do you know it's spruce?" I ask, intending to josh him a little over his outdoorsman knowledge, or lack thereof.

"It's the kind we always get as a Christmas tree," he says, deadpan serious. "Smells just like it."

"Probably spruce, then," I say, moving on to the next lesson. "Okay, time to learn some knots."

We lash the crossbar at about hip height, and then I send him to look for branches to lay along it. "Lots of twigs and leaves still on is good. I'll pile mine on this side; you pile yours on that side. See who's done first."

He seems spurred by the competition, racing back and forth. I take my time since my manhood isn't threatened by losing this "race." I find a small fallen maple at the edge of the copse and drag it back to the site, then strip the branches off one by one. The next time he comes back, he takes his coat off and hangs it on a broken branch before he hurries off to get more.

My way is more efficient, but maybe his way is more fun. For him, anyway. Well, for me, too, since I get to watch him run back and forth. I have a vague fantasy of doing this someday on a tropical island with him in a Speedo. Or even this place in the summer. Maine can be scorching in July.

I've already got my half of the lean-to loosely covered by the next time he returns, and I see he's picked up my strategy of getting a larger piece to break the branches off.

As he catches his breath, the panting sounds like pure sex to me. I swear I'd be able to pick him out of a pack of marathon runners from that sound alone. "Let me show you how to work the branches off," I say.

He steps close and he smells like spruce. I was going to show him how to put his foot against the trunk and break the branches with the grain, but how about later. I take his hand in mine, the one that was so cold this morning, and pull the glove off. I suck in my belly and stuff his bare hand into my pants.

He wraps his fingers around my erection. "Now that is a fine piece of wood."

I unzip and let it loose into the chill air. "I like it firm on the shaft, light on the head," I say.

His eyebrows rise in surprise, like he wasn't expecting this to be a lesson, too.

"Once the pre-come starts to drip, you can circle your thumb—" My voice cuts off as I gasp, a jolt of pleasure running from my cock all the way to my toes.

A handjob sounds so fucking simple. So routine. Kid's stuff. But with my back against an aspen and my breath coming out in great puffs of winter steam, his hand around my dick feels anything but routine. It's so intimate I can't even speak for a while, as he does exactly as I said, gripping hard around the shaft but then barely grazing his thumb through the wetness on top, making my legs shake.

"If you pull on it downward or to the side, I won't come." My voice is breathy and rough and I grip the tree behind me with my gloved hands, hearing the bark crackle. "Has to be—" I can't catch my breath. "Has to be straight up, in the center."

"I can do that." He isn't pulling on me fast, just steadily, and he adjusts the angle so my cock points directly up my stomach toward my face.

But this isn't the place to leave a wet spot, is it? No. "Stop."

He drags his thumbnail across my slit as he drawls, "Are you *surrrre* you want me to st—"

His teasing defiance makes me snap. "I gave you an order!" My hand swings out almost before I can think about it, intending to grab him.

But he's not there. He's dodged away, eyes wide, hands shaking.

My chest is heaving in the grip of an arousal so intense I can barely think. I repeat the words, trying to get a grip. "I. Gave. You. An order."

"Yes, sir," he says, pressing his hands together now, unsure what to do with them. Unsure what to do at all.

"Feet together, arms straight, shoulders back," I bark. "And eyes front."

He knows what attention is even if I haven't said.

I walk around behind him and stuff myself back into my shorts. The pain of being brought so close to release but denied throbs in my crotch.

His obedience makes the throbbing worse. My voice is calming now, but that makes it cold. "When I give an order, I expect it to be followed unless you have a very, very good reason to question it."

"Yes, sir."

"Tell me what you did wrong."

I'm expecting him to parrot back what I just said. His answer catches me by surprise. He's not playacting at all. "I should know better than to be so casual about touching you, especially when you say stop. I know if I said the same that you'd stop immediately. I'm sorry."

Is that why I'm overreacting? Because I feel violated? I don't think I do, but it's telling that he might think I feel that way.

Time to take things down a notch. Defuse the situation with a little humor and get back into scene. I circle him until I can see his face again. "Apology accepted. Now. What did I tell you about needing dry ground?"

It works. He snorts with the sudden release of tension. "It's the most important thing, sir."

"That's right. So making me come all over the place here would be what?"

He's unsure how to answer, but he gamely tries. "A mistake, sir?"

"That's right. A mistake."

I'm a little amazed that Chase can be both bold and hesitant at the same time. He swallows, but instead of shrinking away from me, he asks, "And how . . . I mean . . . What should I do to make up for my mistake?"

I love that spirit in him. "Learn from it," I say. "Now you're going to gather up dry leaves. Make a bed out of them eight or ten inches thick inside the lean-to. And when you're done, I'm going to lie down on it, and then you're going to crawl in and suck me off. And you're going to swallow every drop so we don't leave a mess. Am I clear?"

"Loud and clear, sir!"

Man, he's really into this. He's more fun than a new puppy. I give him a hard pat on the rear. "Get to it, scout."

And off he goes again. I swear I can feel his fingerprints on my dick, even when he's not there.

SEVEN

Time stamp: 1545 Wednesday, Ledge Island

Chase takes the binoculars up to the promontory at sunset. He watches the water; I watch him. I see one hand trembles a little.

"How's your wrist?" I ask.

He lowers the specs. "Hm? Oh, fine." He shakes out his hand. "A little tired and crampy from holding these up for so long. No sign of the whales tonight."

"Following the fish," I tell him, as if I know what I'm talking about.

He keeps his face turned toward the open water in case he catches sight of something. "Hey, speaking of fish, I saw the tackle and stuff in the cabin."

"You want to try fishing?"

"Sure, why not?"

The only time I've fished from the island was in summer, but I'm not sure that makes a difference. "Maybe tomorrow." I check my watch. "Sun's going down."

He rubs his cheeks, which are pink from the wind. "So what's the deal with tonight? The second it sets I'm your captive again?"

"You still up for it?"

He nods.

"Tell me something you hate."

He's not expecting that. "What?"

"Something a trick's done that you didn't want to do again, for example." I feel I'm being charitable by explaining, but I want him to know exactly what's coming.

"Oh, you mean like sticking a flashlight in my ass?"

I raise an eyebrow skeptically. "You let a stranger you met through an app stick a flashlight up your ass?"

He snorts. "I once let a guy I met through an app kidnap me to an island in the Atlantic Ocean."

He has a point. "Yeah, well." Chase's willingness to flout common sense has worked to my advantage. But that little red flag—so little it's the size of a cocktail straw—waves from the back of my mind: it's really up to me to keep him safe.

That's all right. That's what I'm good at.

He obviously feels the need to explain. "Some old guys can't keep it up enough to fuck. But they can jerk off to what turns them on." He shrugs like it's no big deal. "Object insertion is a pretty common fetish."

"But you didn't like it."

The blush on his cheeks deepens. "No."

"Give me the binoculars, please." I hold out my hand, and he hands them over. "If you don't want to be sodomized tonight by the handle of my Maglite, you'll evade me until nineteen-hundred. That's seven p.m. Three hours from now."

"And if I'm successful?"

"If I don't catch you until after nineteen-hundred, then it's just good ol' garden-variety sodomy with this bad boy here," I say, rubbing my crotch. I'm stiffening up merely imagining what might happen tonight. "I'm going into the cabin now to give you a ten-minute head start on your 'escape.'"

"I'm ready." I can see him looking around, trying to decide which direction to go, but he doesn't move. Smart. He's obviously waiting until I'm inside the cabin and can't see which direction he goes.

I latch the cabin door once I get inside, and I unlock the combination box where I've stashed my tablet and the phones. The night-vision goggles and some other equipment are stored there as well. There are two slots for handguns, too, but they're empty.

I make a quick check of my messages. Nothing from Aiden. Okay, fine. Then I spend a few minutes reading up on winter ocean fishing in Maine. Huh. Mid-December is high season for harbor pollock. That was probably what I saw schooling when we Zodiacked in.

I'm so sucked into reading about the damn fish that I give Chase an extra minute unintentionally.

I put the aforementioned Maglite, night-vision goggles, an LED headlamp, rope, a handful of condoms, and some lube into a pack and sling it onto my back. My erection feels huge as I lean over to tighten the laces on my boots.

Time to hunt.

Everyone expects tracking skills to be mostly the ability to read marks on the ground or broken twigs. I think it's maybe ten percent that. The other ninety percent is guessing what your quarry's thinking.

Cass and Ruiz hunted me once like this and DP'd me when they caught me. Before that I hadn't known it was possible to take two dicks at once. I hadn't watched enough porn, I guess. I was such a babe in the woods then.

Now I'm the hunter.

I'm horny and jaunty as I make my way down the path toward the copse where we built the lean-to. It's a win-win situation here, really. Whether I catch Chase before or after the deadline, either way I'm expecting it to be exactly what we want. The sky is darkening fast, but I can still see with the naked eye.

I'm guessing that he probably went this direction, where he got a good look at the terrain earlier. He wandered around quite a bit more than I did. Maybe he'll think that gives him an advantage. Maybe he even noticed a good hiding place nearby.

I can see freshly disturbed leaves, but they're likely from our movements here before. A fair amount of underbrush surrounds the area where our lean-to is, difficult to move through without making a lot of noise. I check inside the lean-to just in case he's decided to make it really easy on me—nope—and then I stand still, listening.

The wind always kicks up around sunset, and the sound of it masks the smallest noises, but if a twig cracked, I'd hear it. There's no animal on this island large enough to break a branch unless you count him and me. There are squirrels and birds, and Cass swore there are fishers and martens, though I haven't seen them.

Something rustles. I don't move. I focus my senses in the direction of the sound. If he panics, he'll run, and that'll make plenty of noise. If he doesn't panic, or doesn't even know I'm there, then he might still give himself away. And if he's not even there, then there's no harm in me waiting for more input.

Nothing. No new sound. I move quietly around the cleared area of the copse.

If he's here, he's staying hidden. I decide to explore the perimeter. A smile breaks across my face as I realize his name is *Chase*. The longer it takes to find him, the more whetted my appetite will be.

Two hours later the night is as dark as any I've ever seen, and although the wind has died down, a chill is in the air. As I breathe in, I can feel the tingle in my nose that means it's below twenty degrees, which means it's going to be even colder soon. I wonder if we'll hit single digits tonight. It's a bit early in the year for a cold snap, but not unheard of. Climate change has made both the highs and lows more extreme.

It's been long enough, I figure. I snap the NODs on and put them in IR mode. The landscape is dark except for a bright spot to my right: a small animal that flees as I approach, its body heat lighting up the scope. Looks like Cass was right about us having fishers on the island, or maybe it was a fat marten.

No sign of Chase nearby. I'm maybe a hundred meters from the cabin on the landward side. I switch from IR to regular night-vision mode and everything goes green. Thanks to technology, I can now see where I'm walking, the tiniest bit of starlight amplified like a floodlight. I circle the cabin along a rocky path.

In any hunt, there are stretches of patience punctuated by moments of anticipation. My ardor might seem to have cooled, but I'm just waiting for a sign. Meanwhile, I walk, I look, I listen. I've got the advantage, and I know there aren't many men more patient than me. If he gets impatient—or cold—he'll make himself known.

That time with Cass and Ruiz, I'd *wanted* them to catch me. I'd wanted to be fucked six ways from Sunday. But I'd also wanted to keep my pride. They hadn't given me a time limit, so I made one for myself. If they didn't catch me by midnight, I considered myself the winner.

Technically, they didn't catch me that time. I gave myself away. In fact, I had to hunt *them* to make sure they'd find me.

I switch back to IR mode and make a scan around me. The cabin shows up bright white, much warmer than everything around it.

My blood surges, my heart pumping and my cock coming to attention with painful suddenness. It takes another moment for my conscious mind to read what I'm reacting to. *There he is.* His outline is barely visible, white on white, crouched against the back wall. I switch the goggles back to regular night mode. He's under a tarp covering the stack of logs waiting to be split for the stove.

I'm amused. He figured the safest place to hide was right under my nose. It might have even worked if I hadn't had the goggles.

I take the long way around to the front of the cabin, considering the next phase of the operation. I'm going to engage.

I stow the goggles in their case and put it into the bag. The LED headlamp I strap around my forehead, but I don't turn it on. Then I quietly set my bag down near the front door. I leave almost everything there.

I take a hank of rope with me. I wait, eyes closed, for several minutes, making sure they're fully adjusted to the dark. Then I feel my way around the sidewall of the cabin. There's enough starlight in the cold, clear air to make out the edges.

There might be a slight crunch of gravel under my boots as I approach the corner. There's no light from inside the cabin, but I can see the regularity of the edge of the tarp. If he's listening hard, he probably knows I'm coming.

I am listening hard. I can hear his rapid breathing. He's keyed up.

I wonder how hard he's going to fight back.

I whip back the corner of the tarp with one hand and hit the headlamp with the other. He's much more blinded by it than I am—it's shining right in his eyes—and he throws up a hand to block the light. That's all the opening I need, leaping on him and getting control of one arm immediately. I let him struggle purely to up the anticipation.

Sweet mother, I forgot what heady foreplay a struggle can be. He twists and strains and the glorious friction sends sparks right through my groin. Every movement of his muscles is the equivalent of a cock twitching in my hand.

I force him to his feet against the wall. His face against the wood, I make a quick tie of his forearms behind his back, each hand touching the opposite elbow, the rope wrapping around his coat sleeves. Yanking him back by the collar of his coat, I get into character. "Did you think you were going to get away from me?"

His plea is high-pitched. "Oh fuck, don't do this to me!"

"Do what?" I growl, pulling him toward the cabin entrance.

He scuffs his feet, putting up token resistance. "I know what you want. Men like you only want one thing."

I laugh. "Oh, you're wrong, fuckhead. You're wrong. I want many things." I shoulder open the door, pull him inside, and push him down onto the bed. "Many, many things."

He swallows hard.

"Your mouth, your ass, that's two right there," I say as I get to my feet. I quickly pull the bag inside and then latch the door. I shed my coat where I'm standing and then get my boots off while I'm talking. "Humiliation, pain, maybe a little blood, an earthshaking orgasm . . . That's four more."

He rolls onto his back and tries to kick me as I reach for him. I catch his foot and force him onto his face or risk a sprained knee. Once I'm straddling his back, crushing his arms a little —enough to immobilize him, not enough to hurt him—I pull his shoes off and his pants quickly follow. There's something undeniably arousing about seeing him half-clothed this way, his legs and ass bare just so I can fuck him.

I smack that ass because I can, and he struggles indignantly.

"Oh yeah, wiggle that ass." I shove a dry fingertip into him and he goes suddenly still, whether because he's trying to defy my words or because of the intrusion, I don't know.

I climb off him, sniffing my finger, intoxicated by his musk. He needs to be restrained.

No handcuffs this time.

More rope. It's the good climbing rope, smooth and black woven through with colors. Part of my brain is annoyed that I don't have two hanks that match, so one arm will have to be done with red, yellow on the other. I unzip my jeans to let my cock breathe a little while I work on him. I'm in no hurry now. His coat has to come off and it's time to tie him in a more secure fashion. I make a gauntlet for each arm.

This particular style of rope tying I didn't learn in Boy Scouts, though a surprisingly large number of the knots are the same.

Or maybe it's not surprising.

When he's kneeling at the edge of the pallet, facedown with his arms spread, each tied to a corner post, I'm ready to start the real mind-fuck.

I lick my index finger and tease at his hole, feeling it twitch and jump. He tries to clench his buttocks together, but I'm kneeling behind him and I shove my knees between his, my cock hitting the back of his thigh. "If I want you open, you're going to be open, boy," I say.

"Oh, God. What are you going to do?"

"Your daddy's going to hate me so much." I can't help but feel a sick thrill at that thought. Aiden probably hates me so much right now that he's giving himself an aneurysm over it.

"He'll kill you if you touch me."

"Oh, it's too late, then," I say, digging the lube out of the bag and drizzling it between his cheeks. I run my finger up and down through the wetness and then jam it into him suddenly, making him gasp. "I've already touched you."

"You know what I mean," he says, taking on a spoiled-brat tone of voice I haven't heard before now. But it quavers as I twitch my finger against his prostate. "If you d-don't rape me, I'll tell him to spare your life."

Oh, that is rich. I laugh deeply. "I'm not gonna rape you, boy," I say wickedly. "I'm gonna ruin you."

The Maglite I have isn't the giant-giant one, but it doesn't have to be to feel like a violation. The barrel of the one I've got is about the size of a dick but as black and metal and cold as a gun. I show it to him, putting the condom onto it with great relish so he knows just what it's for.

I get two fingers into him and can feel him bearing down on them, squeezing and letting go, trying to get himself ready to take it, even while his mouth is keeping up the act. "Please don't put that thing into me. Please."

"Time you learned who's in control here, boy. I can, and will, do whatever I please to you."

I have to be careful not to touch my cock for a little while once I have the flashlight buried a couple of inches in his ass. I might come without warning, the sight is so arousing. So are the pitiful whimpers he makes, pleading wordlessly.

"You want me to take it out, boy?"

"Yes, please, sir—please take it out."

I grasp it as if I'm going to do as he's begging, and I pull it maybe an inch out, then push it back in. When he realizes I'm not taking it out after all, but instead pumping it, fucking him with it, he starts to full-on cry.

Shit. I'm not prepared for tears. Are they real? If they're not, then calling him a sissy is the next obvious line in the script. But if they are real . . .

I don't want to cut him that deep.

Besides, it's been three hours and my cock could not care less about our little role-play fantasies. It wants to be in him. *Now.* "Enough of that," I say, and he gulps, putting a stopper in his tears as I toss the Maglite to the floor with a heavy *thunk*.

The reservoir tip makes a crinkly sound as I rub my cock up and down his abused hole. It's gaping, and I make no attempt to prep him in any way other than to pull his cheeks apart.

I shove in. It's so intense that I feel like my entire body was just hit with a shock wave. I'm holding onto his ass cheeks like the next wave might knock me across the cabin. And then I'm pumping into him. Rough and raw. With the condom there's too much friction to fuck him quickly. But I'm not in a hurry, not even thinking about orgasm yet. The only thing in my mind is to get my cock into him as deep as it will go, claiming him wholly with each individual thrust, pulling back as if the only reason to do so is because I might drive even deeper on the next try.

But as sweat mixes with the lube, the way gets easier, his hole shaping itself to my cock, and before long I've forgotten the playacting, the scenario, and even the real fact that I've kidnapped him, all coherence gone under the force of nature that is the fucking itself. All there is in my world at this moment is fucking Chase, devouring

Chase, molding my chest to his spine as if I could turn us into one being right through the shirt he's wearing.

His voice is muffled by the bed, but he's not saying anything with words right now. His moans are rhythmic, synched to my hips, and I can't tell which of us starts to speed up first.

My fingers are still sticky from the lube. I spit into my hand and snake my arm over his hip, finding a gratifyingly stiff cock. He can't help himself. He thrusts into my fist and I hold steady, letting him ping-pong back and forth between impaling himself on me and fucking my hand. His upper body can't move, tied down as he is, so he's all spine and clenching buttocks.

I clamp down hard on the roar that wants to pour out of me when I come, so all the energy goes right into the tip of my dick—burning, pulsing.

He's not so quiet. His sounds grow frantic as he pushes himself toward climax. If I were really a sadist, I'd pull my hand away now. I'd have some whole other gear to go to, some new plan for torturing him. But I don't. I have four fingers and one thumb squeezing and moving as his flesh drives against them, and then I have the hot release of his passion jetting into my hand.

I keep stroking until his cock goes soft and his rapid panting changes to a groan. My own cock hasn't slipped free yet. I lick my palm and get a nice tongueful of jizz, sating some animal hunger in me that isn't about orgasm at all.

Then my brain kicks in again. I push my hand at his face, remembering the scenario, wondering if he'll refuse, or try to bite me.

No. His tongue tracks the same groove in my palm that mine had followed and then snakes between my fingers, licking up every trace of come.

That night he sleeps on his side with his arm rope gauntlets tying him to one bedpost, with me spooned around him. The fire in the stove burns down to almost nothing, but like that, we're warm.

EIGHT

Time stamp: 0915 Sunday, Ledge Island

Every night, I tie him to the bedpost before we go to sleep to make sure he can't run away while I'm asleep, and I swear I've never slept this well in my life. Every morning, I wake up with his morning wood in my hand. We've spent the past few days working on improvements to the cabin, and fishing and fucking. Chase found the first-aid manual and went through the entire thing yesterday. When he gets back to the mainland, he should get certified easily.

This morning I've apparently been tease-stroking him for some time while asleep, and I reach awareness gradually, the scent of his skin against my nose, the quiet whimpers in his throat, the need pulsing against my fingertips as they brush upward, upward, upward on the sensitive track up the center of his glans.

My own cock is as tense and itching for release as his, trapped against his tailbone. But I ignore it. I wonder how long I've been teasing him. For that matter, I wonder if he's even fully awake. I drag my thumb through the large amount of pre-come gathered at the tip of his cock, and he gasps like he's surfacing from a deep dive. He's definitely awake now.

"Oh jeez, I gotta piss," he says.

"Then I better make you come. No way are you getting anything out through this." I grip his shaft with my slick fingers, and he shudders. "But first . . ." I whip back the sleeping bag we're under, and he cries out from the sudden chill.

I go to build up the fire. Hanging from a line beside the stove are three small work towels that have become our regular come rags over the past few nights. I can almost use them to figure out how many times we've had sex, except I've lost track of how many times Chase has washed them and hung them there to dry. At least twice each, but maybe three times.

And he'll have to once again. I scoot one under his target zone and one under his ass. "You wet this fucking bed and I'll never let you come again," I warn, pulling the sleeping bag over us again as I mold myself around him. "Your bladder must be huge right now."

"Yes, sir!" He's a bit breathless.

"See how this feels," I say, as if I'm letting him try on a sweater. What I'm actually doing is slicking my cock with a combination of his pre-come still coating my fingers and my own spit. And then I'm rubbing the slick, fat head against his hole.

He tenses suddenly. "You gonna put it in like that?"

My half-asleep brain snaps suddenly to attention. *No condom.* It's not like me to forget that. What the hell is this situation doing to me? It's one thing to fantasize about shoving it in there because I can—*I really could*—and another thing to actually do it because I am a fucking idiot who forgot. It's like the scent of his skin drops my IQ.

It's the sleep, I tell myself. After so many years of sleeping with one eye open, something about the cold and the exertion and having him securely tied has lulled me into a deeper sleep than I'm used to. There were so many nights in the past year where I slept in a chair at the hospital or on top of a bed at the motel across the street with all my clothes on, with my ears expecting a dire phone call at any minute. My brain isn't used to real sleep, to real rest.

It just proves how much I need it, how hard the year of my mother dying really was, and how much I lied to myself about what her death was doing to me. Physically, I mean. I know it's deranged me mentally. I know what I'm doing is wrong. Revenge isn't a healthy motivator. But my choices are either enact the retribution that restores my sense of justice, or self-destruct. In the service, risking my life was a given. Choosing self-preservation over other priorities is still foreign to me.

Self-preservation means being sharper than this. "You know I'm only teasing," I say. "Testing you."

He whimpers in acknowledgment, and I go get a condom, glad that, because of how he's tied, he can't roll over to see my crimson face.

I turn away from him while I tear open the package. With the rubber pinched in one hand, I smack my cock several times with the other. Let him think I'm just stimulating it, getting it good and hard, but it's already rock hard and I'm doing it to punish myself. Nothing like a good spanking to make a lesson stick in your mind, hmm? *Stupid, stupid, stupid*, I think as I give myself a few whacks. *You need to be* more *alert than this.*

But I need to fuck him even more. I've been through periods of my life where I had a lot of sex. Hell, there was one deployment where Cass, Ruiz, and Garrett took turns with me every day for a week. Three cocks, two holes, seven days . . . I was sore as fucking hell and I loved it. But I've never had such a relentless need to stick my cock in anything or anyone as I've had since Chase first opened that motel room door.

I get the condom on and lube up. This time I don't bother pulling the sleeping bag over us. The cabin will be toasty warm soon enough. I turn Chase facedown—one of his knees bent, his head tucked against his still-bound arm—and mount him.

The grip of his hole is so perfect right now. He barely needs any preparation at this point other than a single finger of lube to make sure the way is slick. After that I can squeeze my cock right in. Regular fucking has its advantages.

The sound he makes as my body meets his is his pleasure noise, the low wanton cry of a beast. Two animals moving together, mindless in our hunger. So much for keeping alert.

I fuck him slowly a few times and some thoughts return. "How's that feel?" I demand, my thumbs digging into his ass cheeks, pulling them apart so I can see where we join.

"Uh-uh-uh-mazing," he stutters. Grunts. "What did you do? Does spanking your meat like that make your cock bigger?"

"Ha, no. It's your full bladder pressing on your prostate." I slow-fuck him some more.

"It's amazing," he repeats. "I can't even describe it."

"I know what it feels like," I say, admiring the sight of my shaft as it moves in and out of him.

"You do?"

"Hell, yeah. Biggest, baddest topman I know tied me to a showerhead once and made me drink two liters of water, left me there for ninety minutes, then came back and fucked me until I pissed myself."

He sounds wide-eyed, even though his eyes are clenched shut. "Wow. No shit."

"Nope, no shit," I say. "Just piss. If I'd shit on his cock, he would've made me lick it off."

He barks in surprised laughter. "Jeez. That's harsh."

"One badass motherfucker," I agree. Garrett was never completely right in the head, I think. I decide not to tell Chase—yet, anyway—about whose mouth I'd pissed into. In fact, I'm not even going to tell him anything more about Garrett. I've already said too much. "See? I'm nice. I won't make you piss yourself. And I'm gonna let you come."

Let is an inaccurate term. I sink to the hilt and shift so he's on his side again, and I resume the tease-stroking of earlier. I tease and tease and tease until he's jabbering, half-incoherent, begging for a firmer stroke.

The only firm stroke I'll give him is an internal one. Out and in, out and in, and then suddenly he's coming so hard he overshoots the come rag and hits the underside of his own arm with his ejaculate.

Well, it'll be his job to clean it up. I ease out of him and untie him from the post. "Go on, go out and piss, but don't take too long or I might not give you an option you like for how to get me off in return."

"Yes, sir!" he answers quickly, but it's half a minute before his aftershocks subside enough for him to raise his head and move. Once he finally does regain the ability for movement, he hurries to pull on my boots and outer coat but doesn't bother with anything else. It's a good look on him.

When he comes back, I'm sitting on the edge of the bed, a fresh condom in place. I beckon him over before he can take the boots off, and I point to my cock with two downward taps of my finger.

How he knows that I mean for him to straddle me and impale himself, I don't know, but that's what I want and that's what he does. He hasn't even taken the coat off, and the cold clings to it and to his bare ass, a delicious contrast to my hot flesh. When he's fully seated, I wrap my warm hands around his chilly cheeks. "Why do I love fucking you so much?"

He laughs, his forearms on my shoulders. "My ass is magic," he says, still giddy from having come and from the breath-stealing cold I just sent him out in to relieve himself.

"As good an explanation as any," I say, driving up into him. My balls are impatient to empty, and it's time. "Squeeze tight now. *Nngh.* Good b—" I don't even finish the last word as the orgasm grabs me and squeezes me like a giant fist.

Sweet mother of God, I don't want to give this up. The way my heart beats, the way the blood surges through me, feels so good—now I know what people mean when they say they "feel alive." This isn't even pleasure, so much as a whole-body feeling of *rightness*—like taking that first gulp of water after a desert run, or that first gulp of air after a tankless dive. *I need this as much as air.*

And that thought is what steals my breath away.

I can't have Chase Milford. I can enjoy the spoils of my illicit labor a little longer, but no matter how this turns out, I won't be keeping him in this cabin forever. If it all goes well, I'll be giving him back to his father. If it all goes badly, he'll be forcibly taken from me. My face is pressed against his chest, my arms around his rib cage, and I don't want to let go. I want to hold onto this moment forever.

You stupid fuck. This is the one man on earth you can't have a relationship with. For every reason imaginable. *Even if you hadn't just kidnapped him, he's Aiden's flesh and blood, for fuck's sake.*

Fortunately, my badass top persona can hide all that angst by channeling it into being a bit of a jerk. "Off," I bark. "Get cleaned up. My turn to piss."

We fall into our morning routine. We haven't even been on the island a week and already we have a routine. He brings water from the well and gets the kettle going. He mixes me a bucket of warm water. Every day I use a cloth to sponge-bathe my genitals, and then I pass it to him to do the same.

Today when I'm done getting matted jizz out of my pubic hair, I rinse the cloth and am about to hand it to him when I change my mind. "Present yourself," I say.

He's just finished stripping down again. "Sir?"

I point to a spot on the floor in front of me. "Feet apart, hands behind your back, chest out."

He takes the position silently, but I see him swallow in anticipation, wondering what I'm going to do and how much it's going to hurt.

The only thing it could hurt is his dignity, I think, and Chase doesn't seem to have any of that to begin with. Not with me, anyway. I start to wash his flat stomach, ridding him of the streaks of dried lube, then work on his thighs, eventually to his cock and balls.

I rinse out the cloth again. "Turn around and bend over."

I take my time cleaning him up and enjoying him, memorizing him, his ass, the furrow between his cheeks and the peach-fuzz globes. "Clean as a whistle," I say, patting him on one butt cheek to signal I'm done and he can stand up.

He straightens and looks at me. "What does that even mean? How can a whistle be clean or dirty? Well, okay, it could be dirty if you mean like . . ." He gives one of those "hey baby" whistles.

"I dunno. Just something my dad used to say."

His eyes narrow a fraction. I'm hoping he heard the past tense in that sentence and isn't going to ask me if he's still alive.

He does ask a question, and it isn't the one I'm expecting at all. "Do you take after him?"

Best defense is a good offense, sometimes. "In some ways, probably. Do you take after your old man?"

He snort-laughs. "Not a chance. Not in the slightest. Obviously." He gives me a funny look, like I should know that.

Except he's not supposed to know that I know that. Sweat prickles at the back of my neck.

No, wait, he told me the whole bit about having a homophobic jerkwad for a dad. That's obviously what he means. I force my inner threat-level meter to reset. "Obviously," I say. "Okay, scout. Thaw some fish out of the stock box and make us some breakfast."

I could really use a good run right now. We get dressed side by side, and I'm thinking over where I could go. The trails aren't very well worn since no one's had a chance to wear them in and there are no deer or large animals to make tracks. From here to the copse where the lean-to is isn't bad, though, low on rocks and underbrush, and along the ridge to the watch point is rocky but clear enough if I goat-step it. I've been doing a couple hundred sit-ups and push-ups a day, but I could really use something more aerobic besides sex.

While he's getting the pollock we caught from the cold storage outside, I tuck the burner phone into my pocket.

"Where you going?" he asks as I jog in place to warm up my legs outside the cabin door.

"For a run. Be back by the time the fish is done." I stand on one foot and stretch my quad.

"Okay." He leans over and surprises the hell out of me by kissing me on the cheek. I'm so surprised I laugh, and he does, too.

I know I'm supposed to ruffle his hair right now—probably after putting him in a headlock—and treat it like a big, fat joke. But my masculinity isn't feeling particularly threatened right now, and the laugh is sweet.

I take off into the woods at a light jog. I can't really go any faster than that. Even circling the lean-to in the copse where there's little underbrush, I still have to be careful where I step. It's a decent-enough workout, but I don't really get to clear my mind the way a long, repetitive run would.

Up on the watch point, the wind is whipping fiercely. It's sunny and clear right now, but the wind chill is fierce. I jog back into the copse to use the phone.

There's a reply from Aiden. This one sounds much more like the cold, calculating man I know, a man who is used to valuing human life in dollar increments.

I've been advised to transfer you the money and get my son back safe. However, I have also been advised to first acquire proof from you that he is still alive. I have also been advised to give you half of the ransom money upon receipt of that proof, and half after his safe return. $2.1 million in the first transfer awaits your proof that he is alive. The remaining $2,070,131.29 will follow as soon as he is safely released into my custody.

Seeing the exactitude on the calculation makes the hairs on the back of my neck prickle—proof that he knows it's me and he knows why I'm doing this. What other research has Aiden done on me besides the exact amount of my mother's unpaid medical bills? There shouldn't be much to find at this point...

I switch over to the weather app to glance at high and low tide times for the upcoming week. Sunset at 1555 tonight. Chance of snow in a couple of days. My mind is on Chase, though. Aiden wants proof that Chase is alive? What kind of proof should I send? If I ask Chase to make a video or something, I'll have to tell him the truth.

Think it through, Eric, says a voice in my head that sounds a lot like my dad's. *Haste makes waste.*

I jog back to the cabin. Inside I find Chase crisp-frying the pollock after coating them with salt. When he's done, we eat them right off the bones like cobs of corn, holding them in slightly singed fingertips. His lips are greasy and salt-laden and taste like satisfaction.

"I wish we could stay here forever," he says when I pull back from devouring him.

Hope rams itself down my throat and makes my heart stop painfully. "Do you?"

"Yeah. I mean, think about it. Would *you* want to go back to living under my father's roof?"

I shrug to hide the twister of emotions knocking everything over inside me, trying to figure out what to say. "This place isn't really made for long-term living," I hedge.

He looks around as if what I've said is a bit too obviously inaccurate—*c'mon, it's a bunker for holing up indefinitely post-apocalypse*—but doesn't call my bluff. "Yeah, I suppose we'll get tired of eating fish eventually." His voice holds a bitter note.

I try to kiss it away, to tell him without words that I'm not the least bit tired of him, that I'm not rejecting him. Not in the slightest. I'm rejecting the impossible notion that he might actually mean forever, that he might actually mean staying with me.

I don't completely succeed. He acts placated but still seems somehow ruffled underneath as we go about our day. Today we're caulking cracks to keep drafts out of the cabin. We easily hauled in enough pollock to feed us for a week or two, assuming it stays cold enough to keep them frozen, which seems likely given how this December has been going. He's right that we might get tired of eating it. Might have to get creative with the canned goods to add some variety . . .

No, I think. *No*. I'm about to send Aiden some proof that he's alive, after all, and after that it should all be over pretty quick. We won't still be here weeks from now.

Chase isn't the only one who wishes we could stay on this island forever, but wishes are just a way to wound your future self with promises you can't keep.

"You know, we should do this at night," he says. "One of us could be outside with a flashlight and one inside to see where the light shines through."

Huh. "That's a good idea." At least, it sounds like one. We'll have to try it to find out. Later. I'll need to remember not to just tie him up right away when it gets dark. Maybe if we make love now, I think, I'll be more patient tonight.

Having thought of it, I now instantly want it. I want to make love to him just for the pure joy of being with him, knowing full well our days together are numbered. "Hey, come here."

He puts down the caulking tube and comes over to me. I'm standing by the front door. He looks up at the metal pipe bolted into the lintel. "What's that for? Bondage?"

I snort. "Pull-ups. The only reason I haven't been using it is the door has to be open when you do it, and that'll make it cold in here."

He has that cheeky look in his eye. "You've never tied someone to it?"

"You're the first and only hostage I've brought here," I say. "Can't say what the other guys may or may not have done with that bar."

"You've never been tied to it, either?"

I curse inwardly for having kindled his curiosity about the other guys. "No. My days on the bottom are long over."

He sucks his lower lip into his mouth and when he speaks again, it's plump and wet. "I hope mine aren't."

I slip a hand around his waist and pull him against me. "You sure? For me it was . . . a kind of apprenticeship. A way to prove myself."

"Yeah, true," he says, his hands sliding under my shirt to my bare skin. "I'm not saying it's not that, sometimes. With you especially. I . . . I really like being tested."

"So I've seen." This close I can smell the wood smoke in his hair.

"You were okay with the . . . the guys? . . . putting you through it?"

"Yes, I was okay with it."

"Even though you're not a bottom?"

"I was a willing participant in all of it, if that's what you're asking," I say. "And I think dividing the world into tops and bottoms leaves out a whole lot of people."

"Okay," he says with a nod. "Okay. I hear what you're saying. But bottoming is not a phase I'm going through, if that's what *you're* asking."

"Good. Because I love fucking you so much," I say, rutting against his hip bone. "And I want to right now."

"Yes, sir," he whispers as he turns his neck aside for me to hickey my way from his ear to his shoulder.

Before long, I've flattened him against the bed and I'm taking my time rubbing my erection against his through our clothes.

His hands settle on my biceps. "How many push-ups can you do?"

"Many," I say, then trace a tendon in his neck with my teeth until he squirms upward against me. "Got pretty close to a hundred in two minutes before they would even look at me to go to boot camp."

His eyes flick toward the bar over the door. "And pull-ups?"

"Twenty-five." I'm holding myself above him now. "Why all the questions?"

"Curious, I guess." He pumps his hips upward, making his dick graze mine in a hell of a tease. "It's hot how in-shape you are."

"All it takes is time," I say. "Anyone can make themselves strong physically with repetition. Mentally strong? That's another story."

He pushes his pants down and rubs his bare erection against my crotch. "Did the guys you talk about make you mentally strong by . . ." He hesitates. "By what they did? Fucking you in the shower and that kind of thing?"

My instinct is to deny it, to say, *Hell no, we were just horny as fuck.* Not to mention bored and sometimes stupid. If anything, all the power sex games bonded our team emotionally more than they affected us mentally. But I can hear a note beyond mere curiosity in Chase's voice. He's seeking something.

And who's to say my mental toughness wasn't improved by those games? Or that Chase's isn't being built up every time I challenge him?

These thoughts sweep through my mind at lightning speed, and I nip at his mouth while I choose my answer. "You're already mentally strong," I say. He has to be or he'd have cracked before this.

"You think so?"

"I know so. Or you'd be begging me for less, not more." I sit back on my haunches to undo my fly. "It's why it's fun to push you. If you were weak, I'd worry about taking you too far."

"Yeah?"

"Yeah. Instead I mostly worry that we're both going to be so chafed from constant sex that neither of us will ever recover."

He snorts with laughter. "I'm doing okay so far."

"See if you still say that in an hour," I say. "Because my number one plan is to make my cock at home in your ass."

"Yes, sir," he says as he exhales.

I do fuck him for what feels like an hour. Long and slow. No talking, no tests, no power games. Just me giving and him taking. My attention goes no further than the nest of our discarded clothes. Chase's skin is all that matters, and the sounds that he makes as we join, and the way the blood pumps through my chest.

We fuck until I come. Taking my time like that, it happens slowly, but when the orgasm bubbles up, I don't try to stop it. I let it build, sweet and slow, until it shakes loose, ripping free of me with a sudden harshness of breath that feels surprising given the gradualness of its approach.

Chase holds me in place, all his limbs wrapped around me, keeping me from withdrawing. He's breathing hard, too, but I can feel his cock trapped between our bellies, hard as a pistol grip. "That was—"

"Not over yet. You next."

He hums in anticipation. I disengage from him gently and then put his own underwear over his eyes as a blindfold.

I suddenly know what proof I'm going to send to Aiden. "Stay still."

"Yes, sir," he says, breathless but obedient.

I tie his wrists to the bedposts with rope, then his ankles, spreading him across the bed in an X. I aim the cell phone camera up one leg, capturing his throbbing erection and his blindfolded face in the same shot. I add a video to the collection of still photos, a few seconds of his cock twitching. No doubt that he's alive.

Here is your proof. He is alive and well. I promised I'd keep him safe and wouldn't hurt him, and unlike some people, I keep my promises. You have my word he'll be returned to you whole and healthy if you meet my demands. Make the deposit and I'll tell you where to find him.

The video trickles into the internet. The cell phone signal is weak here and it fluctuates, sometimes disappearing and then reappearing. I play with Chase's balls with one hand while I monitor the phone in the other. He's more patient than I am, lying there content to let me tease me endlessly, while I can't wait for the damn upload to finish. Eventually it goes, though. There, Aiden. There's your proof that he's alive and well, with all his limbs.

I'm jubilant that the operation is proceeding as planned, but my gut twists at knowing that soon this will be over.

I'd best savor him as much as I can. I take his cock in my mouth, and the salty tang of his pre-come makes my mouth water.

NINE

Today it's above forty-five degrees, and in the sun the weather feels, as they say, "nice." We finish the last of the caulking from the outside now that it's within the temperature window for the stuff, and then celebrate after lunch by sunning ourselves on the promontory rock like lizards. Even at midday the sun is on its winter slant—weak, but it still feels life-giving after the cold snap. When the wind starts to whip up, we head back into the cabin.

"What's for dinner, scout?" I say.

He folds his hands like a waiter, his heels together. "Tonight's menu: your choice of beef stew from a can, fish, or ramen noodles."

"You found ramen?"

He shrugs and makes his hair stand up when he runs his fingers through it. I think he has no idea that he looks like a grass stalk gone to seed when he does that. "You didn't say I couldn't look through the storage bins. I was surprised to find some in there. I'd think bugs or rats might chew into them."

"I'm not sure there are rats on this island, but there are chipmunks."

He looks hopeful. "Maybe we should eat it before something else gets it?"

"You like ramen?"

"You don't?" Those two words seem to open up a million questions, depending on my answer.

I press on instead. "When did a rich boy like you eat ramen?"

"Everyone eats ramen noodles," he says, moving to the bin where they're stored. "It was something I could make for myself before I knew how to cook. Something I didn't have to ask a nanny or a nursemaid for. First it was the kind in the cup, and then I moved on to the kind you make in a pot."

"Which kind do we have?" I ask, as if I don't know. As if I didn't take the last few packages out of my mom's nearly empty cabinets when I cleaned out her house, as if I didn't bring them here because I couldn't bear to let them go to waste.

"The kind in cups," he says, producing two Styrofoam Cup Noodle packages. "I know we won't eat for a while, but I'll fill the kettle."

"Not much protein in ramen," I say, but my objection is as weak and slanted as the winter sun.

"I could make some fish, too." He gives me that shrug again. "And know what I saw at the watch point today? Wild chives."

That makes me smile. "Onion grass?"

"What you call onion grass is actually a kind of onion, you know," he says. "I'll go pick some. It's kinda freeze dried, but it'll taste good on ramen noodles."

I sit on the edge of the sleeping pallet. "Ramen," I say.

"Yeah." He sounds confused. "That mean you're saying yes?"

"*Ramen.* Not ramen *noodles.*" I can hear my mother's voice in my head, chiding me age four or five when I asked for my favorite food. I'm not trying to be a hard-ass, but I can't help it. "That's like saying 'noodle noodles.'"

He winces. "I know, I know, so they said at culinary school, if you want to be technical about it. But I guess you like to be technical about most things."

I nod. So true.

"But are we having them or not, regardless of what you call them?"

I stretch out on the bed, trying to sound as laid back as my posture. "Sure. Go fill the kettle and pick your onions or whatever so we'll be ready when it's time to eat."

He bounds out the door like a puppy let off the leash. I find myself smiling again. I might have to admit I feel happy when I've smiled twice within five minutes. It tells me how happy I could have been if Aiden hadn't fucked with my life.

Or if I hadn't fucked with Aiden's life. But if I hadn't done that, I wouldn't have gotten to know Chase like this in the first place.

Or would I? If I'd gone crawling to Aiden to beg for my old job back after he'd let my mother die . . .? Would I have been assigned to bodyguard Chase on trips to his culinary school?

I have to wonder. Generally speaking, Aiden had kept me and the rest of "the muscle" away from Chase—was it because he thought we might do something inappropriate with his beautiful angel of a boy? And was that why once he found out for sure I was gay, he had to get rid of me?

What Chase said about a bodyguard driving him to and from culinary classes gnaws at the back of my brain. Too old for a nanny at that point. Did Aiden even let him learn to drive a car? That mansion really was a gilded cage, a soft prison.

Chase returns with the water and greens, and preps the meal for later, whistling while he does it. From my vantage point stretched out on the bed, it feels decadent to have him serving me. Is this what Aiden feels like every day, an emperor with servants scurrying to do his bidding? My years of employment with him certainly lead me to think so.

I can't lie still while Chase works. I sit up and search for something to keep my hands busy. I dig my boots out from under the pallet and look them over. There's one pair for using in the water and one for running overland. They're both in fairly good shape right now, but if I don't maintain them, I know I'll run into trouble eventually. If we ever come back here long term, we should add more clothing and shoe-repair supplies to our pack list.

Chase sits beside me while I stow them back underneath. Then I quickly reach for him.

He flinches away, and my heart fucking breaks, my hand falling as limp as some other parts of me. *Words, Eric, words. Use them.* "Are you . . . all right?"

"Oh, just . . ." His gaze is on his lap, head tilted downward in shame.

"Just what?" I'm suddenly alarmed, and that makes my voice sharper than the nurturing tone I'm trying for. I reach more slowly toward him this time, unsure why he's—I'm—we're—suddenly so fragile. My fingertips make cautious contact with the flannel on his shoulder, but I move incrementally to let the weight of my hand settle there. I resort to whispering to make my voice soft. "Just what? It's okay. You can tell me."

Under my hand I feel the tension begin to notch downward. "I don't want to let you down. I want to be … you know, ready, whenever you need me."

He's talking about sex, but those same words could've come out of my mouth any number of times when I was a young recruit. I know how to handle this one. I've been given this speech. "I had a chief petty officer tell me once in no uncertain terms it was my job on the squad to hump the fire hoses during fire-training week. I wrenched my elbow on the second day and didn't tell him. I thought it was my job no matter what. Didn't want to let him or the squad down."

"What did you do?"

"Suffered. Made it worse. Made myself an ineffective part of the team. Because I didn't do what I should have first, which was tell him I was hurt. It wasn't my job to decide that an injured sailor should keep trying to do a job he wasn't fit to do. That's his job. So I made it impossible for me to do my job *and* for him to do his job."

He looks up at last. "Yeah, but … having sex with you isn't a job."

We're tiptoeing through a minefield, and I have no idea what we might be about to set off. "Then you should be even more honest with me."

He's still hesitating.

"Honesty is very important to me." I can barely say it without cringing, knowing all I haven't told him. I try to make it make sense. "You don't have to tell me anything you don't want to if it doesn't affect us." *Us? Since when is there an "us"?* "But if it's making you flinch, I should definitely know. I thought …" I swallow my fear that I'm about to step wrong. "I thought you liked it when I hurt you."

His cheeks go scarlet and he can't meet my eyes. "I do."

"Your hand and wrist doing okay?" I'm still angry at myself for the handcuffs.

Chase turns his hand over as if to show me it's fine. "It was only numb that one time. But … other parts of me aren't doing so well." The way his voice drops when he says, "I'm *sore*," tells me exactly which part of him he means.

I put my hand on his shoulder as relief sweeps through me. Physical damage is much easier to heal than psychological. "Didn't I just say the other day I was worried about us getting chafed from constant sex?"

"I thought you were joking. I mean, I didn't think it was even possible."

I squeeze his shoulder gently. "Just because I was joking doesn't mean we shouldn't take it seriously."

He's still treading cautiously. "You're not disappointed?"

"I'm never disappointed when you trust me." It's the right thing to say, but I still feel like I'm stabbing myself in the gut. "I love fucking you, but there are plenty of other things we can do."

"Yeah?" He's brightening up fast.

"Yeah. Strip and I'll show you."

I don't undress, just get my cock out, and then I lie back on the pallet. When Chase is naked, I coax him into straddling me with his ass in my face. He's about to receive the gentlest rimjob I can give while he sucks me until I come.

This is something I've never had before—someone to care for. I never had a little brother or even a subordinate lover. The closest I had was Mom, at the end, when I couldn't really do anything for her, couldn't actually protect her or heal her hurts. But I can take care of Chase, and with each soothing swipe of my tongue over his swollen flesh, I feel the urge to care for him growing stronger. I blow on the wetness and feel him wriggle, and then I have to lie back because the sensations reaching me from my own cock become overwhelming.

He hoovers the jizz right out of me, swallows to leave no mess, and then serves up as loving a tongue bath to my softening cock as I gave to his other end.

I pat him on the butt cheek twice to tap out and he stops, crawls around to lie beside me. I beckon him into the crook of my arm, and he pulls the sleeping bag over us. He makes a contented hum even though he hasn't come.

"Mm-hmm," I agree. When have I ever felt like this? Like simple affection is something so present, so huge? Possibly never. We lie still together, his bare skin pressed against my clothes, my arms around him, and it's even more intimate than fucking him.

I don't know how long we lie there, quiet and warm, with no anxiety or urgency forcing me to move. It's a foreign feeling, but I enjoy the newness of it, the strangeness of it.

I surprise myself by being the first to speak. "So, ramen tastes like independence for you?"

He shifts in the crook of my arm, and I wonder if he had drifted to sleep. "Yeah, I guess it does. What does it taste like for you?"

The problem with asking questions is it invites questions. I don't want to tell him how much Cup Noodle I ate while my mother was dying. I tell him a different, older truth. "My dad used to tell me a story. He was stationed in Japan for a while and there was ramen everywhere, but the guy who invented the instant ramen in the cup? He was a national hero. After the devastation of World War II, people were hungry. He wanted to invent something people could eat anytime, anywhere, that would give the nation the strength to survive tough times. Cup Noodle was the invention."

"Wow."

"Yeah. I used to make a tent in my room from a blanket and pretend I had survived a war and sit in it and eat Cup Noodle."

Chase chuckles. "And you grew up to be the guy with the bunker in the woods with a stash of Cup Noodle."

I have to laugh, too. "Yeah. I guess I did."

His next question is more cautious, another tiptoe onto the minefield. "You were close with your dad?"

No, we weren't close. I idolized him, but we weren't close. We didn't get a chance to be close. "He was killed in action," I say. That usually closes the conversation right there.

Not with Chase, though. "How old were you?"

"Five."

"Was he a SEAL, too?"

I am suddenly done with questions. "If you don't let me up to piss, I'm going to soak you in it." I've freed my arm and I'm getting my boots on before he can object. I can't help but shoot back, "How'd you know I was a SEAL? I never said that."

He cracks a smile. "Oh come on, after the way you talked smack about the Army Rangers at your Boy Scout camp?"

I bark out a laugh. "Yeah, okay." It just goes to prove that no matter what you're trying to hide, you can't be other than what you are. I slap him on the bare thigh. "Come on, piss time, and then dinner. Sunset's coming."

TEN

Time stamp: 1530 Wednesday, Ledge Island

No reply from Aiden. It's been over forty-eight hours since I sent the proof and still no reply. I'm getting antsy, no other way to put it, but I'm trying to keep Chase from feeling it. When I'm edgy, though, I'm tough. I've been working him over pretty good for two straight days when night falls. We're standing at the watch point looking for whales, but the sky has darkened early with clouds. He points across the dim water to something unmistakable, a colorfully lit party boat of some kind. It's one of the only vessels we've seen in over a week that we've been on the island. Most likely they're on a pleasure cruise of the coast, but my hackles rise as I wonder if it's an elaborate cover for a SWAT team or worse.

"Some kind of corporate Christmas party," Chase says, looking through the binoculars before handing them to me.

I look, too, wondering what he's seen that makes him think that. As they draw nearer, I can make out people dancing through the windows of a party deck. The faint sound of a live band playing "Jingle Bell Rock" wafts across the water followed by the sounds of the boat's engines as they pass near the island, coming about in the deep part of the bay before heading back out again.

"Can they see us?" Chase asks.

"No. We're in the dark to them." They must have a navigational chart that tells them not to come too far into the bay or they could run aground on our island or any number of others. "The only way to get their attention would be by radio or flare."

"Do we have a two-way radio?" he asks.

It doesn't feel right to lie to him. "There's one in the storage chest, along with batteries, but it's useless if there isn't someone listening on the other end."

"That's deep," he says with a smirk. "Hey, I've lost track. How many days until Christmas?"

"Some," I say. It's December 20th. I'm kind of counting on Aiden wanting his boy home for Christmas. If he does, he's running out of time.

"Well, Merry Christmas," Chase says, and puts his arms around me. He kisses me on the cheek, sweet as a Starlight mint, and I feel a momentary flush of warmth. Momentary because a second later my stomach twists again with the realization that very soon this has to end. I don't deserve this affection. It's all an illusion, and he'll see that the moment I tell him.

The words stumble out of my mouth like a badly practiced lie. "M-Merry Christmas." Does he think a kinky pickup is turning into something more? *You stupid fuck, he better not be falling for you.*

"You know what I want for Christmas?" His breath is warm in my ear.

"What?" I ask automatically, trying to hold myself perfectly still in his embrace, as if that could calm the rough waters churning inside me.

"You'll have to catch me to find out," he says.

A second later he's sprinting away from me, down the flat face of the rock and into the dark woods. I'm frozen for a few crucial seconds while my brain gets in gear, and then I laugh out loud, partly in glee, partly in relief. He was just lulling me with that moment of affection so he could take off like a wild thing.

Oh, yes. It's so much better to slide into my hunter persona than to stand here being eaten alive by my worries. He wants to be chased? The chase is on.

I run after him, into the same gap in the trees he disappeared into, but I won't try to catch up to him in the dark, even if in my fantasies I simply run and run until I tackle him to the ground, tear open his clothes, and fuck him on the spot. My blood pounds at the thought, but no, that's not how we're going to do this. I'm better trained than that. I head toward the cabin and the night-vision goggles. The Boy Scout motto is "Be Prepared." I put the lube, some condoms, and a flashlight into my jacket pockets, some other stuff into a light pack on my back, and off I go on the hunt.

I'm not anticipating that it'll take long to find him. I'm anticipating another long, warm night in the cabin. His ass is sore, but I didn't let him come earlier. Maybe tonight will be the night I milk him mercilessly, forcing as many orgasms out of him as possible. With the NODs in IR mode, I follow the glow of his heat-emanating form through the trees. I stalk him past the lean-to copse and toward the northern tip of the island.

I'm not anticipating that as he hears me coming on the path, he's going to break into a run again.

I'm not anticipating that as I run after him I'm going to turn my ankle, but that's what happens. My foot goes into a hole, and down I go with a grunt. Fuck. I get myself righted and feel my ankle through the leather of my boot. Seems okay. I should've known better than to run in the dark, though. Infrared doesn't show you the terrain. And Chase, what was he thinking? He could've stepped in this same hole.

I look around. The glow of him is gone. Time to continue the hunt.

I circle back to the lean-to to check inside it. Nope, not there. I stand at the entrance to the lean-to, listening, watching. Twenty or thirty meters west I see a fisher or something like it scurry away.

Then I see the glow. I switch to night mode to make out the outlines of the trees. The fallen spruce. He's in the natural shelter under it.

A natural shelter that isn't easy to escape from if you're larger than a fisher. I move as silently as I can, the wind through the trees masking the sound of my boots against the dried needles underfoot, until I am almost there. I memorize the shape of him, crouched under the horizontal trunk, and then stow the NODs. I set my pack down. The only thing in my hand now is my Maglite.

I'm on him in a hot second, one arm around his neck, the other pressing the cold metal end of the flashlight against his temple. He freezes when he feels it.

"Is that a gun?" His voice is harsh, every word a gasp.

"Keep struggling and you'll find out," I say.

He goes limp and I loosen my hold. He's still on the ground, knees tucked under him, head down. I press the "barrel" of the flashlight against the back of his head, and he asks, "What are you gonna do?"

"Punish you for running away, of course," I say. "Can't have my captive thinking there's no consequences for trying to escape."

"O-okay." Fear or excitement makes his voice quaver.

"You sore, boy?"

A hesitation before he answers. "A little, sir."

"Then my cock will be punishment enough."

"Oh, God," he says, but my blood surges at the note of desire in his voice. He's breathy and trying to stay on script, but it comes out terribly insincere when he adds, "Anything but that."

"Anything? You'd rather I fuck you with the flashlight again?"

He backtracks quickly. "Er, please, sir, I won't do it again. I won't run away again. I promise."

Huh. This is an interesting twist on the game. "You promise?"

"Yes, yes."

I undo my belt buckle. "See if you still want to keep that promise when I'm done with you. Get your pants down."

I click on the light, and he keeps his eyes shut. He's on his knees as he pushes his pants down as far as they can go and then bends over again.

If we weren't in the middle of the spruce, if we were in the open, I'd whip his bare ass with a branch. Some other time. Right now the only thing that makes sense is this.

I examine his hole with the light. It's less red and swollen than it was the other day. The rest has really helped him. I lube up one of my fingers and press it slowly into him.

The groan he gives is pure sex, no protest at all.

The words in my mouth won't stay locked behind my teeth no matter how hard I try. "Good boy," I say, stroking his hair with my other hand. His hole clenches around my finger.

"Am I?" he asks, then catches himself. We're off script. He tries to get back on. "I mean, if I'm good, does that mean you won't hurt me?"

I push another finger into his hole. What does he want? Does he want me to say yes or no? He gets off on being forced—I'm one hundred percent sure of that—but I can't tell if he's trying to change the deal here or reinforce it. "You're my captive," I say, trying to roll with it. "You do as I say, you stay put, I'll treat you well."

"Yes, sir," he says, and his voice doesn't sound the slightest bit fearful. He sounds fuck-drunk and I haven't even fucked him yet. I kiss him on the back of the neck, grab a hunk of skin in my teeth, and bite just enough for him to really feel it, then kiss the spot again.

"But you ran, so here's your punishment." I'm not planning to come now. I'm just planning to teach him a lesson. "My dry cock."

"Oh, God," he says again, arching his back to angle his ass toward me.

It's not actually dry, of course. He's well-lubed, plus I'm leaking pre-come like crazy. I swipe the bare head up and down in the wetness, teasing him.

"Oh, God, *please*," he groans, and I can hear what he means by those words. He's begging me to put it in right like that: bare, raw, wild.

"Right like this," I say. I want nothing more than to have my flesh join with his, no barriers between us. "I'm taking you right here, right now."

He reaches back and pulls at my leg needily.

I wrap my arms around him from behind and push and push until I've speared him on my cock.

"Oh, Eric," he gasps, and I freeze. Was that what he said? Was that my name? He doesn't *know* my name. "Oh, fuck. Oh, fuck."

He didn't say *Eric*. He said *fuck*. But adrenaline pours through me from what feels like a close call as well as the utter thrill of barebacking him like this. The wind in the trees is picking up, roaring through the canopy, and the scent of spruce is intense as I bite him on the back of the neck again. I pull all the way out and then push at him again until his body lets me in. "You're mine, boy."

He whimpers and starts to tremble. "Yes, sir!"

"I think you like being mine." This doesn't feel like role-playing anymore. I rock my hips and deepen the penetration. "I think you like it when I fuck you like this."

"I do! Fuck, it's so good!" It doesn't sound like role-playing anymore, either. "So good."

"What do you want?" I hear myself demanding it as I begin a rhythmic thrusting. I'm way off script. "What do you want?"

"This!" he screams. He's pushing back against me, squeezing my cock as hard as he can, speeding up the rhythm. "Oh, God, this! Fuck me, take me, rock me."

And I do. I'm fucking him hard now, extremely hard, the light on the ground beside us as I grip him with both hands, driving my cock into him as deep as it'll go. When he starts to scream again I don't stop, and it takes me a while to realize that the reason he's screaming is because he's coming. I've never fucked a man so hard he came like that, but I reach around to feel the evidence for myself, catching the last few spurts of his come in my hand. I pull out, smear my cock with it, and jam it back into him. It only takes a few more thrusts before I'm adding my own semen to the mix and my own howls of lust to the rising wind.

ELEVEN

Time stamp: 1645 Wednesday, Ledge Island

I am so spent that I literally stumble back to the cabin after that. We've got spruce needles in our hair like some kind of wild things, and our clothes are only partly redone as we fight to shut the door against the wind. It's starting to feel like serious weather is coming in. When I stand back, the latch rattles in the gusts. Can't really batten it like the hatch of a ship. I push a storage trunk against the door instead. "Good thing we finished that caulking," I say.

"Yeah."

I turn around to see Chase has stripped to nothing. He's shivering but he's standing straight. There's dirt on his face and under his fingernails.

"Good boy," I say. "Stoke up the fire so you're not cold, and warm some water so I can clean you up."

"Yes, sir." The Boy Scout and the captive have merged into one role. One fuckable, irresistible role. Like something from a dream, from my wildest fantasies.

I get out of my clothes, too. Everything's a little damp, and Chase hangs it all up to air out and dry, then treats the semen spots as best he can. We do the same for ourselves without an actual shower.

I'm exhausted. I want to collapse into bed with him in my arms, but I know I should check the weather.

And see if there's a reply from Aiden.

I beckon Chase under the sleeping bag, and I feel my eyes drooping despite the urgency gnawing at the back of my head. "You sleepy?" I ask.

"Not really. Can't sleep through all this noise." The wind is like a train going by. He snuggles against me.

"Here. Try this." I slip from the bed to get a bandanna. "A blindfold will help you sleep."

"It's my ears, not my eyes, that are the problem." He sits up and chuckles. "You know, if you want to blindfold me, all you have to do is say so."

A flutter of nerves comes out in my laugh. Of course. I stick to my course of action, though. "Just try it."

"All right." He lets me tie the cloth around his eyes and then lies down on his pillow. I don't need to tie him tonight, and part of me misses it a little.

Maybe I was onto something with my blindfold idea, though. He falls asleep within minutes. I get out a phone to check the weather.

Snow and wind are both in the forecast. Lots of both. As I look beyond the pat icons in the app, I see it's a nor'easter bearing down on us. Great.

I start putting my clothes back on. Aiden can wait. I've got things to do before the snow starts coming down.

Chase lifts his head immediately. "You all right?"

"Fine. Snowstorm's on the way. I'm going to secure some stuff outside and bring more wood in here."

"I could help."

I climb onto the bed and nuzzle his hair. "No. You stay right here. If we get snowed in, I'll want you well rested for the workout your ass is going to get."

He wiggles back against me. A massive snowstorm never sounded so good, eh?

The wind is serious, whipping and gusting hard enough to nearly knock me off my feet as I move the wood. The rest of the woodpile I try to protect with the tarp, but if a corner works its way loose, a wind like this might carry it all the way to Canada. The first fat, wet flakes start to fall just as I'm refilling our water containers. Wind-driven snow stings my eyes as I make it back inside and shut the door again.

"Every time you open the door, the heat gets sucked right out by the wind," Chase says.

"Let's try not to open the door too often," I say. "I'm planning to piss in the old stew cans."

He laughs. "If we have to."

"Wouldn't do to have your dick freeze off." I shed my coat and climb onto the bed with him, kissing the back of his neck and then grazing his ear with my teeth. "I like it too much."

He murmurs assent. Before long he's drifting to sleep again, though, and when his breathing switches to a quiet wheeze, I go to check for a reply from Aiden. I crouch by the lockbox and get out the phone. It takes a while to connect. I wonder if cell phone service is going to be knocked out by the storm.

The first thing I check is the account where the money should land. My heart begins to hammer as I see the balance. The Bitcoin exchange rate fluctuates some, but there's no mistaking that nearly two million dollars are now sitting there, waiting for me.

Two mil sounds like a lot of money. It is, when you consider that it should be enough for me to live off the rest of my life. But it's not when you consider that it was only half of the cost of the treatments my mother needed.

He paid. Aiden actually paid. I feel light-headed for a moment. This means he accepted the proof that Chase is alive. Now to negotiate the handover.

I check the messages. There's nothing from him. That seems odd, but maybe the money was his message. I send one to him.

Money received, thank you. This will be my second-to-last communication to you. You have 48 hours to pay the rest. When I receive the amount still due, I will inform you where you can pick him up, whole and healthy. That will be my final communication.

It takes a while to type out the message because my hands are shaking. This isn't like me. I'm known for being cool under pressure. I've been in plenty of live-fire situations, but I guess none of that compares to delivering the comeuppance to the asshole billionaire who let my mother die.

I can almost still hear his voice, the way it echoed in the large, empty dining room where he told me. When he gave me orders, it was usually in his study or in one of his vehicles on the way somewhere. This time, though, he called me to the dining room, a huge parlor of a room with ten-foot-high glass French doors every few feet that opened onto an equally large patio. I assume now there was a sniper out there ready to shoot me if I reacted badly. Surely he'd hired my replacement already before firing me, no?

"Eric, we have a problem," he said, sitting at the end of the extremely long table in the only chair in the room. "A very big problem."

I said nothing, waiting for him to tell me what this was about. I stood across the corner of the table from him, my back to the glass doors.

"Some information has come to light recently that disappoints me greatly." He was speaking in a quiet voice, but with all hard surfaces in that room, every word reverberated slightly.

I still said nothing. I had no inkling at that point that he was speaking of me. Not until he pushed a folder toward me, across the flawless varnish of that dining table. I flipped it open and the first thing I saw was a photo of Garrett and Cassidy locked in an arm-wrestling battle at a bar in SoCal. I didn't have to look any further to know that whatever else was in there was a lot worse than arm-wrestling.

"Your entire squad was kicked out of the Navy," he said, voice as cold and even as it had been all along. He was wearing a suit but no tie, his shirt partly unbuttoned, his watch and rings glinting in the light of the chandelier overhead. He had let his hair grow a little in the back, going gray but slicked back for an aging man's vanity.

"With all due respect, sir," I said, "it was my fire team, not my squad." Four men, not eight. I don't know why I bothered to correct him. I didn't know where the conversation was going. I thought I knew my boss fairly well by that point. It had been almost two years since I'd saved his life. I knew he was greedy and craven, but I thought taking a bullet for the man meant something to him.

He was shaking his head slowly, as if in disbelief. Or censure. "'Mentally unfit'?"

"Technically the term is 'medically unfit,' and it was an honorable discharge." As if Aiden gave a fuck whether my discharge was honorable or dishonorable. "You knew I was a section eight."

He clucked his tongue and took a pack of cigarettes out of his jacket pocket. "I knew you were crazy. I didn't know you were a pervert."

The file told him all he needed to know—and more—about just how perverted four men could be. He flipped open the file again and made a show of paging through, then closed it in disgust. "Says here they could've got you pervs on everything from fraternization and conduct unbecoming to adultery." He gave a low, appreciative whistle. "I didn't even know the military gave a fuck about adultery. Learn something new every day. I guess they really wanted to get rid of you and your buddies."

I've always wondered, if we'd managed to stay in until the repeal of DADT, would the same fate have awaited us? Oh, probably. After all, Cass, Garrett, Ruiz, and I weren't merely gay. We were banging each other in various inappropriate situations. And that was just for a start.

"It's a high-stress job," I told him.

He tapped a cigarette against the table and then flipped open a metal lighter. "Like working for me isn't?"

"With all due respect, sir, working for you, I've only been shot at once."

Again that deep chuckle. I wasn't feeling too much stress at that moment, not more than usual, though I was a tad nervous. Aiden liked to play games, holding back information until the moment he chose to reveal it to you. He liked to bust people's balls and yank their chains. It was what he lived for. I tried not to take it personally most of the time. "So. You're a pervert."

"Excuse me, sir?" I always called him sir. It was easier than learning a new habit.

"Kinky as fuck, if what I'm reading here is at all true." He raised an eyebrow, daring me to refute it. When I said nothing, he took a drag on the cigarette and blew the smoke in a bluish stream right at me. I'm not a fan of cigarettes and he knew that. "Unbuckle your belt."

"Sir?"

"You heard me." He leaned back in his chair, as if this were a nonchalant request.

"I don't do that kind of thing anymore, sir."

"Do it for me," he growled, flicking cigarette ash onto the floor.

Consent is a slippery damn thing sometimes. We were locked in a battle of wills. I wasn't ashamed of what I'd done in the military, and I wasn't shy about showing my body. But I didn't want to do as he said. It felt like if I did, we were about to cross some kind of line. "Sir—"

"It's just a little thing, Eric. After all I've done for you?"

He had made sure my mother was seen by the best oncologist in the state, given the best care at the most modern, state-of-the-art facility available. He had unhesitatingly assured me that as long as I was a member of his family, he would take care of her as if she were part of his family, too. I was grateful, but part of me had been wondering if another shoe was going to drop. Maybe this was that shoe.

Maybe Aiden Milford was a kinky fucker, too, and he'd waited all these years to show it? Waited until he had proof I was twisted, too?

Or maybe he just felt he owned me now. Now that he'd spent so much on my mother's care. My skin prickled as that thought settled. "Sir, I told you, I don't do that kind of thing anymore."

He appraised me coolly, his gaze raking me from knees to chest as he took another slow drag on the cigarette. "Your dick is having other thoughts." He shifted his own crotch, as if the sight of me had given him a boner. "I can see the bulge from here."

He was right. He was tapping into all the reflexes that told my cock to snap to attention when a man in charge said jump. I wasn't about to let him know that. "With all due respect, sir, my dick gets hard when the wind blows."

"And in high-pressure situations, eh? Am I pressuring you, Eric?"

A direct question requires an answer. I kept my mouth shut, trying to wait him out.

When he didn't get his way, he resorted to insults. "Oh, come on. Don't pull that 'inscrutable Chinese' shit with me, Jackie Chan."

I knew we'd definitely crossed into new territory of some kind when he said that. He'd never used racial epithets with me before. Never mind that I'm half Japanese (other half Scottish), not Chinese. Insults don't have to be accurate to burn. I felt my cheeks redden. When was the last time I'd let a racist remark get under my skin like that? Junior high? I counted to ten as I inhaled slowly, trying to force myself to be calm. I was never into humiliation play to begin with; actual humiliation was something I had no idea how to handle.

"Tell me, Eric," he said, flicking the metal lighter open again. "Do you like pain?"

"No, sir," I said, my eyes on the flame.

"What would you say if I said I wanted to burn you on the dick?"

"I would say, 'No thank you, sir, that isn't my cup of tea.'"

"I want to burn you on the dick, pervert."

He feinted toward me, and I snapped into a defensive stance faster than he could blink.

"It's poetic, you see," he went on, snapping the lighter shut and then opening it again, "because I'm *firing* you."

"Excuse me, sir?"

"You're fired. I was prepared to believe this so-called report was nothing more than a pornographic fantasy. A manufactured conspiracy against four good men. But it's obvious it's true." He clucked his tongue again as he got to his feet. "Such a shame. I truly thought you were something special, Eric."

I didn't dare take my eyes off him or move.

"As of this moment, your employment with me is terminated. Unfortunately, with termination, there go your benefits as well. I expect you to be off the property in under fifteen minutes, or I will have you dealt with as a trespasser. It would be a shame to shoot you."

At that point he walked out of the room, trailing a blue cloud of smoke as he went. I smacked my idiotic boner, burning with humiliation and tamping down the edge of panic. I knew that by *benefits* he meant Mom's treatment. But what could I do? All I could do was leave. I took the file and got out of there before he decided he wanted to exercise his sadism some more.

TWELVE

Time stamp: 1007 Thursday, Ledge Island

The morning comes but no dawn, the storm still raging. The sound of the wind is threatening, as raucous as a mob. I concentrate on breathing, on feeling the air move freely in and out of my lungs. Chase is pressed against me. The cabin is chillier than usual for a morning: I can see my breath. Even with the caulk job, there are drafts when the wind is like this.

Chase lifts his head, and before I can say anything he has sprung into action, stoking the coals in the stove and adding new wood. Then he burrows under the sleeping bag with me once again. "Brrr. Snow in December is usually nice."

"The whole White Christmas thing, you mean?"

"Yeah, you know. If it's been bitter cold, it usually warms up toward the freezing point to snow." He puts on a falsetto voice. "And then the snow comes down placid and silent, blanketing the world in peace and beauty." He snorts at the end and I smile. "Not this time, I guess."

"It's a nor'easter," I say. "That's kind of like a snow hurricane."

He laughs. "I grew up in New England. I know what a nor'easter is. What about you?"

"Didn't I just tell you what it was?"

"Ha. I mean where'd you grow up." He settles his head on my shoulder. His hair still smells like spruce.

"My dad was in the Navy, so we moved around when I was little. Hawaii, Florida, Texas. After he died, we moved to New Jersey. I guess to get away from where he died or some shit like that." I'm suddenly restless and start thinking about finding a can to piss in.

"I thought you said he was killed in action?"

Can't sneak anything past this kid. "In a training exercise, actually."

"I'm sorry."

"It was a long time ago." The wound feels fresh for the first time in decades, though. My fists clench and I try to force myself to relax. It's been so long since I thought about this, but as I lie here with him, there's nothing blocking the memories from flowing. "My dad's swim buddy came to the house to console my mother. She'd gotten the news while I was at kindergarten and she hadn't told me yet. I answered the door and the second I saw his face, I knew."

"Oh, man." Chase's hand on my chest is soothing.

I can still remember being barefoot and running on the stone tile of the foyer, my feet slapping noisily as I hurried to the door, thinking it was my father coming home. Wrong. "He was a big dude. Even bigger than my dad. I remember punching him in the chest with my little fists, I was so angry that my dad was being taken away." Tears sting in the corners of my eyes, and I can't believe I can still feel that pain so many years later. I blink to clear them.

"He let you beat on him like that?"

"Like I said, big dude. Probably didn't even feel it." Or maybe he did. "When he got sick of it, though, he caught both my hands in one of his—that's how big he was." I remembered the feeling of his huge palm, warm and a little damp, and the mixed scents of alcohol and cigarette smoke from his breath when he spoke to me. "'Save your rage for your enemies, little buddy,' he told me. 'Save your rage for your enemies.'"

Chase's voice is gentle, even if his questions probe deep. "Is that when you decided to become a SEAL?"

"Probably? I don't remember a time when I didn't want to be a SEAL." I stretch my shoulders. If I don't get up soon, I'm going to go nuts. "Thirteen years later I was doing the exercise that killed him."

"Wait, thirteen years later? Weren't you five?"

"I enlisted at seventeen." The Navy knew my story. Recruiters were supportive of my ambition, even if my mother was ambivalent.

His voice rises in disbelief. "You could do all the crazy shit like two hundred push-ups a minute at age seventeen?"

"A hundred in two minutes. Don't exaggerate." It's like I told him. All it takes is time. I got an early start. "You don't become a SEAL overnight. It takes a while." Being focused helped me do it faster than the average Navy recruit, though. "A lot of the time they want you to go to college first, but they liked what they saw in me."

"How old are you now?"

Too young to have both parents dead. "Twenty-nine."

"Seriously?" He heaves himself up so that both his hands are flat on my chest, and he rests his chin on them. "You're not just saying that because every thirtysomething wishes they were—"

"I'll be thirty in February," I say evenly. "You know how I feel about lying."

"That means we're only seven years apart." He blinks, assimilating this information. "That's . . . cool."

I can't help but smile. We're closer to eight years apart than seven, but it seems impossible we're that close in age. It's like time travel. The first time I saw him he was a scrawny, underdeveloped kid. I was a veteran of two combat tours, starting my first bodyguard job. I glimpsed him a few times that year, but then almost never after that. Aiden kept his family very separate from his business. We'd been worlds apart.

"The older I get," I say, "the shorter seven years seems."

"No kidding." He chuckles and seems determined to lighten the mood. "So what are we going to do today? Fuck, I hope?"

That's a change of subject I can get behind. "I thought you were sore?"

"The time off did wonders for me. I was fine last night, especially with no condom." He wags his tail like a puppy, then stills as his voice turns serious again. "You weren't really mad at me for running off, were you?"

I stroke a hand down his back. "It was a fun game for a while," I say, trying to pick my words carefully. "But I like you better right here."

He nods, his chin digging into my chest as he does it. "I thought I was going to love being a brat and being forced. That's what all my fantasies were about. I mean, I *did* love it. But I didn't expect I was going to find something I liked even better."

"Which is?"

His cheeks go adorably pink. "All the obedience stuff. Training. Learning from you and being, you know, tested and praised and rewarded."

I've got him pinned on his back and I'm kissing him before he can draw another breath. I pull back and lick my lips. "There's plenty more I can teach you."

"Good," he says, and rolls his hips upward. It's obscene how sexy he is, naked under me, utterly available for anything I desire, hard or soft, fast or slow. Maybe it's knowing that outside the whole world has stopped for Mother Nature, and we're not going anywhere for a while. *My* whole world has narrowed to him and this moment. How we got here and where we're going next don't even enter my consciousness.

I have the taste of the truth in my mouth. "My name is Eric," I say.

He laughs as if I've told a good joke, like he's slightly giddy. This isn't the reaction I expected. His next words are even more surprising: "I know."

Icicles stab through me. *What?* "You know?"

"Errric," he says, like he's savoring the taste of my name in his mouth.

But I've been so careful. The disorientation makes me feel like we're on a ship, like the pallet under us is pitching in a storm. "Did I forget to take a name label off one of my things? Was it the—?"

He's still grinning. "Eric. *No.* Did you really think I wouldn't recognize you?"

And now I almost feel seasick. My head is spinning, fear and tumult howling through my brain like the wind outside. "You can't," I say stupidly.

"I can." He's frowning up at me now. "You didn't really think a goatee was enough to fool me, did you?"

I don't know why I'm arguing when he obviously knows what he knows. My heart is pounding like we're about to parachute behind enemy lines. "We barely laid eyes on each other when I first got hired. You were just a boy. I can't have left that much of an impression."

His gaze is intense. "You think I wouldn't remember the most beautiful specimen of a man I ever laid eyes on?"

The flattery rankles. My hands are around his upper arms before I know it, pressing him back into the bed like I'm going to shake some sense into him. "Don't joke about that."

"I'm not joking. Eric, don't be thick. You were like my best wet dream come to life."

My mouth feels dry. I can't listen to this. I can't hear it. It's too much.

"I used to fantasize—"

"Stop." I do shake him. My jaw hurts from gritting my teeth. "Just . . . stop."

He grits his, too, and snarls because I'm hurting him by not playing along with his little fantasy. "If anything, I thought at first you didn't recognize *me*. I'm the one who's changed the most."

Shit shit shit shit. All the scaffolding I'd erected to keep up the charade is crashing down with every word he says, and my brain can't keep up with it all. "So . . . you thought I didn't recognize you, and I was inviting a random boy toy to a deserted island? And you went along with it?"

His facial expression shows he's stung. He twists like he wants to get out from under me and I let him, feeling absolutely nauseous about holding him down like that. He pulls on a pair of pants, and I can't say I blame him. I wouldn't want to be showing off my junk to my kidnapper either.

When he speaks, his voice is fragile. Taut. "'Went along with it.' You knew it was me. You *invited* me."

This is where lies will get you. You dig a hole halfway to hell and when it collapses, you're all the way there. "It was . . . safer. For both of us. If you came willingly."

He shakes his head, presses a hand to his face. He pulls on a shirt. I'd get dressed too if I weren't using every scrap of brainpower trying to understand what's going on. I'm sitting up with the sleeping bag bunched in my lap.

"Safer," he says and shakes his head again. "Do you mean to say if I didn't go willingly you would've forced me to come here?"

Yes. That he's even asking this question drives home how successfully deceptive I've been, and yet I can't tell whether I fooled him or myself more. "Chase—"

"You said my name!" He whirls and points at me accusingly. At first I think he means I don't have the right to call him by his first name, but then he goes on, and I realize he means something else entirely. "Back at the motel. God! I thought you were giving me a tip-off! I thought you were making sure, just when a stranger would have been starting to get freaked out, that we weren't strangers at all."

My blood runs cold. "The motel." My lips are numb.

"The second one. I thought—" He breaks off, starting to hyperventilate a little. "I thought that was your way of telling me this wasn't a real kidnapping. That you were doing it because you . . . you . . ." He puts a hand on his stomach. He's starting to look as ill as I feel. "Because you *liked* me."

Oh, fuck. I'm torn between wanting to comfort him somehow—*how?*—and wanting to end the argument as quickly as possible. "Chase—"

He's hugging himself, shivering as the realization hits him. "Oh God. Father always warned me about kidnapping. Oh God." He pulls a coat around his shoulders and shrinks down where he is. I want to go to him, to hold him, to comfort him, but I know I don't have that right anymore. Tears start to brim in his eyes. "Fuck you for proving him right. Fuck you, Eric."

"This wasn't how it was supposed to go," I say, as if that matters, as if there's any defense I can mount for my crimes.

He throws the jacket at me in a brief moment of tantrum and then seems to force himself to go to the stove to stoke it. He's crying silently, his chest rising and falling, but he makes no audible sobs. Not loud enough to be heard over the wind, anyway. He puts boots on and pokes at the coals while my brain scrambles for what to say to fix this situation.

But I know there's no fixing this situation. There's only damage control. "I promised Aiden I wouldn't hurt you."

He stands bolt upright, wiping the tears off his cheeks with the backs of his hands. "How much did you ransom me for?"

"Chase, I'm sorry—"

"How. Much."

I have no good reason to lie to him now. None. "Four million and change," I say. It's shredding me inside to see him cry, tearing at the lizard skin I've accrued around my heart over the years, proving that it's paper thin, after all. "Chase, please—"

"Please, what? You shit. You utter shit."

I can't argue when I agree.

"You seriously thought I didn't know who you were?" The cabin has never seemed smaller than when he begins to pace back and forth as he rants, a caged animal. "You thought you were fooling me into thinking you were just a hot trick, a hot lay? And I let you beat me. I let you bruise me." His outrage comes out a roar: "I let you fuck me with that fucking flashlight—!"

I'm together enough not to say, *But you like it*, even if I can't stop the thought from flashing through my mind. He's exactly right.

"And the whole time *you* knew the only reason you had me here was for four million fucking dollars." He throws up his hands.

"Not the only reason," I say.

"Oh, right, four million dollars and *to fuck me whenever you wanted*."

But I like you. The little voice in the back of my head is as much an idiot as the rest of me today. "I've told you the truth."

"Oh, don't pull that honorable semantics bullshit with me." He comes close, looking down at me with a pitying expression on his face. "You think that matters? You think if I go back and replay every word you ever said and they hold up to some nitpicky definition of 'truth,' I won't be angry anymore? That isn't how it fucking works, Eric."

"Yes, it is," I hear myself say. The problem with ripping away two decades' worth of emotional armor in a matter of minutes is I'm left with the coping ability of a heartbroken five-year-old. Fuck. "Yes. I own it. I intended to kidnap you, and I was willing to capture you against your will if necessary. But the truth matters, Chase. Honor matters. It's the only thing that matters anymore."

He snorts. "Oh, really? Is that how you're going to get yourself to sleep at night? By convincing yourself you upheld your principles despite—" He gestures around the cabin like he doesn't even have words to describe the situation we're in. "All this?"

I don't have words for it either. "Look. I'm sorry. My intention wasn't to lead you on. I didn't even intend to have sex with you at all. Not even the first time." *But you more or less leapt onto my dick.* I'm sure my face is as red as if I'd chugged a half bottle of Jack Daniels. "I never wanted you to get hurt. Only Aiden."

Chase's laugh is bitter. "You know he doesn't feel it when you hurt me, though, right? Not that my fuckwad of a father doesn't deserve everything he gets."

"He doesn't deserve you." I've said it before I can filter it.

"Damn right." He lets out a breath. "I guess we have to wait until the storm's over to get off this rock."

I nod. "When he finishes the transaction, I'll hand you over to him."

Chase blanches for a moment. Then his ire surges again. "You've got to be fucking kidding me."

I hold out my empty hands, like I'm making a peace offering. "Okay. Okay. I won't wait until then. I'll hand you over as soon as—"

He bites down on my name. "*Eric.* Don't be stupid. I'm not going back there."

"You have to." I shake my head. "I made a promise."

"You're kidding, right? You'd really deliver me back to him?"

"I keep my promises."

Chase balls his fists. "I promise you're full of shit!"

The gap between us is widening with every passing second, the flood of emotions washing us further out to sea. All I know how to do is cling to my convictions. "If you want to run away from home, that's your business. But if I don't put you back where I found you—"

"If you don't put me back where you found me, you're *as bad as a criminal*? Is that what you mean, Eric?" He's laughing and crying at the same time.

The forethought and planning part of my brain has been trying to kick back on this whole time, and a thought finally cuts through: *I should've tied him to the bed last night.*

Yes, I should've.

"Sorry, Eric, but I can't do that," he says, and then before I realize what he's doing, he's shoved the trunk away from the door, flung it open, and is out in the snow.

I leap from the bed to go after him, and a moment later I'm on the floor of the cabin, wind blowing snow onto my naked skin, as I clutch at the ankle that gave out. Fuck, that hurts. Much as my instinct is to just crawl after him as fast as I can, going buck naked into a nor'easter is not going to happen. It takes me a minute to scoot across the floor on my butt to shut the door so at least the snow isn't getting in anymore.

Assess. The firefight's over. Assess, damn you, assess.

My ankle doesn't look swollen until I compare it to the other one. *Remember when you stuck your foot in a hole yesterday, asshole?*

I make it back onto the pallet and try to stand more slowly. Nope. It won't bear my weight at all. *Remember stumbling back to the cabin last night?* Apparently I wasn't simply love-drunk. Having a high pain tolerance has never been a drawback.

Until now.

Fuck.

THIRTEEN

I don't have a lot of time to lie around feeling sorry for myself. Time passes while I wait for the pain in my ankle to drop below the level of anguish I'm feeling in my chest, and then my survival instincts kick back in. Chase Milford—whom I'm sworn to protect no matter how much of a stupid fuck either of us is—is out there in a nor'easter.

And let's face it. It's not for Aiden's sake that I want to make sure he's okay.

It takes approximately forever to get clothes on. But not even the drill sergeant in the back of my head that sounds a lot like Garrett can make me move any faster. Neither can the skeptical voice that sounds a lot like Cassidy: *How you gonna handle the fact you can't walk, son?*

I'm going to get my boot on as gently as I can and then lace it as tight as I can stand, that's how. This isn't my first rodeo. The last time it was the other ankle, but I made it out alive, and so did Ruiz.

Of course, that time it was men trying to kill us, not the weather, but challenges are challenges. Maybe the cold will help the swelling go down or keep it numb. Maybe that's why I didn't feel it last night.

Assess. Maybe he'll come back when he realizes how cold it is. I can hope, but I can't plan on that. I try standing slowly on my ankle now that it's laced in. The pain is ugly but I don't fall over. Good.

I open the door. Good thing the wind comes from behind the cabin, or there might be a snowdrift so deep against the door I'd be stuck until spring.

It's only been minutes but in the blowing snow, Chase's tracks are already obliterated, even with over a foot of accumulation out there.

The wind is gusting this way and that now, no longer a full roar, and I wonder if that means we're on the tail end of the storm. It's been snowing for at least twelve hours, but I'm not about to go back in to check the weather report. Now that I've pushed the pain in my ankle to the back of my mind, my only thought is, *Find Chase.*

Find Chase. Find Chase. Find Chase.

I decide to check the watch point first. Maybe I'll find him there still angry but ready to talk more. I visualize it, trying to make it come true as I make my way through the snow. I wonder how much daylight is left. It's gray and dim from the clouds and could be any hour. My imagination plays tricks on me. Is that one of his boots? No, a bit of rock outcropping sticking up through the snow along the ridge. What if he walked along here, lost his footing in the snow, and fell to his death? I try to remind myself just because I can barely walk doesn't mean he can't, but a gust buffets me and makes my stomach plummet.

The promontory is empty, scraped free of snow by the scouring wind. I crawl to the edge to look over, but there's no sign of a body below. Okay, so he didn't come here. I'm desperate to find him. I head back down off the ridge into the trees. Would he try to get to the Zodiac?

Would he abandon me on the island with no way to get off? At least until summer, when the water would warm up enough for me to swim to shore. Still. It's no less a fate than I deserve.

Would he try to pilot the Zodiac in storm-churned waters alone?

Thoughts like this keep distracting me, my focus wavering like a gunsight in a drunk's hand. I get turned around in the snow, and I'm suddenly not sure where I am. Every direction is the same, and there's no good way to navigate in the gloom and continuing precipitation. All the trees look familiar and unfamiliar at the same time. Some are down that probably weren't before—that's how strong the wind has been.

I find the trail down the cliffside toward the beach. Okay. That orients me. I know this place. A sudden worry hits me, though: what if the Zodiac blew loose, whether because Chase tried to get it out or the raging wind just sent it flying? I make my way down the trail to check on it, the rocky face on one side keeping me on track. The snow here is deep at first, but then as I round the cliff edge, it drops to nothing on the sheltered side.

I am goat-stepping down the trail, trying to smother the panicky feeling that makes my hands shake, when my bad leg slips on the ice. The rocks are invisibly slick, and I go down hard onto my ass and slide rapidly down the hill. I have a split second to register the Zodiac is right where it should be while my body is tobogganing toward a beach that isn't there anymore. At the highest of high tides that beach disappears, but the storm surge has submerged it completely in churning waves. I'm grabbing for anything I can.

I manage to latch onto an exposed root with one hand, but I feel my bad shoulder shredding as my legs plunge into the water, my ankle bashing against the cliffside in a wave. I'm in up to mid-thigh, and the cold feels like a vise crushing my legs. But at least I've stopped moving. I'm not dead or drowned. Yet.

The tendons in my arm scream—or maybe that's me—as I haul myself upward, out of the water and onto the rocks.

Assess. Can I make it back to the cabin? Only one way to find out.

I wonder if Chase is going to live through this.

I wonder if I'm going to live through this. But the panic is gone. Clarity sets in when there are no decisions to make. The only thing to do is take one careful, limping step at a time up the path. One step, and then another, and then another. I stop trying to analyze what I know about frostbite and hypothermia and simply focus on moving. I lose track of time passing.

The snow stops, the wind abates, and night falls.

When my legs quit working over the top of the ridge, I start crawling. I'm not that far from the cabin, I think. I can crawl that far.

But then I come to a series of deep drifts and my strength starts to give out.

The voice I hear in my head isn't my father's or Garrett's or anyone's but my own. *Keep going, you stupid fuck. What good is it if you can do a hundred push-ups if you can't crawl the last hundred meters? Chase needs you. You can't give up now.*

Of course, when I could do a hundred push-ups was before I took a bullet in the shoulder. Before I spent months on end in a hospital, sitting still at Mom's bedside. Before I lost my innocence. Before I lost my will.

No. My will is the one thing I haven't lost. My arms have decided they won't move anymore. My legs can barely push me ahead. I remember something I said to Chase not too long ago. If you're wet, you're dead.

Maybe I deserve to die, but I'm not ready to give up yet. There's only one thing left I can do. And that's cry out his name. The snow seems to swallow sound, but under a clearing sky I scream his name toward the moon.

FOURTEEN

Time stamp: 1122 Friday, Ledge Island

It takes me a while to realize that what I'm staring at is the ceiling of the cabin. The day is bright and I have no memory of how I got here. Hypothermia-induced amnesia? Seems likely. When I sit up, I'm dizzy. I can see that I'm alone.

I'm naked under the sleeping bag, and the air is warm from the stove. I can almost believe the whole thing was a bad dream except for the bandages. My ankle is crisscrossed with first aid tape and my toes are bandaged. I count them and am somewhat surprised to find they're all there. I'm almost ashamed of the relief that sweeps through me. My toes mean nothing compared to the more precious things I could have lost in my stupidity and the storm. Chase has to be nearby.

My clothes are all hung up to dry the way he would have hung them, and shame crisps my edges again. I wonder how I'm going to apologize to him, or if he'll accept it. A bottle of water sits beside the bed. I sip carefully at first, then more quickly as it strikes me how dehydrated I am. My dizziness ebbs as the water seeps through my system.

I can see the lockbox is open. I ease my way over to it, trying not to put weight on my ankle, but my arm won't hold my weight either, so it takes a while. None of our phones are in the box, only the tablet, which is useless to me without wi-fi.

I wonder what the fuck happened between me crawling in the snow and now. I'm going to assume Chase heard me screaming and brought me in here . . . and then what? Convinced me to call for help? Or to check the weather? I must have given him the phones.

I remember the sudden fear I had that he'd try to take the Zodiac on his own. I'm much more afraid of him drowning than I am of being stranded on this island.

I test my ankle. It won't take all my weight, but if I'm careful, I can take baby steps. If I lean on something, I can almost walk. I get dressed and search the cabin for any more clues about what happened while I was out cold. The knives and most of the bondage gear are gone, too, and now my skin really starts to prickle with fear. I know he's gone, but I'm trying to imagine that he's not. Maybe I'm wrong. I'm often wrong, right?

He's left me a pair of binoculars and all my cold-weather gear. Outside the cabin the sun is so bright I have to put shades on, or I can barely see from the glare off the snow. Once I do, though, his footprints leading to the beach are obvious, more evidence of what I already know. He's fled.

My chest aches like I've been shot.

I turn a branch into a walking stick. I go along the ridge toward the watch point. My hope is a stupid, fleeting one—that he hasn't gotten so far away that I can't get one last look at him.

One last look.

My heart leaps into my throat as I crest the ridge and the buzz of an outboard engine reaches my ears. I hurry as best I can onto the windswept promontory where only minimal snow and ice clings to the rock. It's a challenge to get my shaking fingers to focus the binoculars, but even before I do, I know I'm not looking at Chase. There are two men in a Zodiac, and it's coming toward the island.

I have no doubt they're coming for me.

I can hide. I can fight. Or I can give myself up. If I hide, I have no doubt they'll be able to find me—I'm in no shape to keep running, and the snow makes me easy to track. If I fight, it's all too likely someone's going to end up dead. No one deserves that just for taking Aiden Milford's money. I didn't get into this to kill anyone.

I go back to the cabin. I've got probably just enough time to close things up before they arrive. Maybe longer if it takes them a while to locate the landing beach.

I prep the place for another long vacancy as best I can while hobbling around, the buzz of the Zodiac's engine reaching me every so often. They circle the island completely, probably looking for the best landing site. That gives me plenty of time to secure the outer latches on the cabin and limp down to the beach. I'm waiting there when they arrive, wondering if they're just going to shoot me on sight.

They don't. I recall Aiden's message about hiring SEALs as I watch them beach the craft, the same one Chase escaped in. At least one of them knows how to handle a Zodiac, anyway. They're both bigger than me. One has his firearm drawn as they approach me.

"Eric Sakai-Johnson?" the other one asks.

"Yes."

That's the extent of our conversation. They tie me up to drag me back to Massachusetts, but they don't shoot me. I half wish that they did, but I know that's heartbreak talking. That feeling like you want to die when you realize you've lost something—or someone—you loved.

I have a lot of time to think while lying there in the back of the van. Three or four hours back to the Milford mansion. Most of what I'm thinking is how stupid I was. Clarity comes too late for me to do anything about it. I don't regret making Aiden suffer. What I regret is involving Chase in the first place. I hope he gets over what I did to him. I hope he's far away from here. In hindsight, I know how much of an idiot I was to think he'd want to go back. How many times did he tell me all he wanted was to escape from Aiden?

I'm untangling the layers of lies in my mind, and I keep finding new truths. Chase thought I knew that he knew who I was. Chase didn't think I was "kidnapping" him. He thought I was *rescuing* him.

And I was going to give him back. Why? Because I'd promised I would. To a man who doesn't respect promises in the first place. It wasn't my honor I was stroking with my puffery about promises— it was my fucking ego.

I haven't felt this red-faced about being naïve since Hell Week. Was my so-called honor actually more important than the living, breathing man I hurt? No, it wasn't. Yeah, sure, without principles, without loyalty, without an idea bigger than ourselves to devote ourselves to, we're nothing more than killers and thugs. Once upon a time I would have killed for my country. Now I'm not sure there's anything I would kill for short of saving Chase's life. Not even to save my own life. After all, there's no one to miss me now.

The only ideal bigger than a man that I still revere isn't God or country or keeping promises. It's love. It's the biggest bitch on the planet. Only love could've made me hate Aiden so much I went after revenge. Only love can make me regret so deeply all the pain I caused Chase.

I feel ill as I remember the look in his eyes as he realized I'd been lying to him. That I'd been fucking him under false pretenses. That none of the things—even the true ones—that I'd actually said or done could be believed anymore. If I'd been trying to destroy a man from the inside out, I couldn't have planned it better.

Please be okay, Chase, I pray to whoever's listening up there. *Forget me and move on.*

Clarity. It's such a strange thing. From where I'm lying in the back, I can see the color of the sky changing as the sun sets, but I can't see any detail of where we are. One of the toughs in the front seat says something to the other that makes me realize we're close to the Cape, though: "Fuck Route 3. Go down 24 to get around this traffic." And it hits me I probably have an hour or less left to live. What's Aiden going to do? Slap me on the wrist, tell me I was a bad boy, and let me go? Not likely.

I don't want to die. When I'm faced with the actual thought, my survival instinct kicks in again. I did some questionable things in Aiden's employ, but I never killed anyone. And I can't believe an ex-SEAL would kill another ex-SEAL. Aiden, on the other hand, would probably have no compunction about putting a bullet in my brain if he thought he could get away with it.

I've already erased myself from the grid. Assuming he gets rid of my body thoroughly enough, he can definitely get away with it.

I have to try. The two of them are still arguing about which highway to take. "Hey, up there, I gotta hit the head."

They go silent, but there's no other response. I don't actually have to piss. I'm just trying to get their attention with some Navy jargon. I try again. "I promise, no trouble. Don't need a meat gazer."

The one in the passenger seat sticks his head into the back. Good. If only one of them was a SEAL, my money's on him. His hair's mostly short except right at the front where he has a few dirty-blond curls. "At least wait till you get out of the van before you piss yourself."

I don't have a lot of time to make an impression. "Were you Team Four? I was in Little Creek—"

"Meat wants me to think he was a SEAL," he says to his partner.

"He was a frog hog from what I heard," comes the reply. In other words, a SEAL groupie. Very funny, Aiden.

I forge ahead. "Where'd Aiden find you? He has a thing for veterans down on our luck."

Curly laughs. "You don't look old enough to be a veteran, son."

"Enlisted as soon as I was old enough," I say. They both look ten or fifteen years older than me. "And was kicked out right before they nuked DADT."

"Gay. Told you," the driver says.

"What else did Aiden tell you about me? Did he tell you I took a bullet for him?"

Curly shakes his head and turns to face front again, trying hard to ignore me now. I have nothing to lose. I keep talking. "I did everything that man asked me to right up until he fired me for being gay, no reason other than that."

"Shoulda walked away and kept going," the driver says.

"He'd promised to pay my mother's medical bills. Hooked her up with special doctors, oncologists, experimental drugs, the whole nine yards. After he cut me off, he cut her off, too. Left us millions of dollars in debt. Left her to die."

Stony silence.

"And she did die. Did he tell you that's why I kidnapped his kid?" I leave out the part where I wasn't actually planning to pay the four million to the insurance companies and hospitals. "I know you're wondering why the fuck I would do something like that. That's why. Aiden Milford killed my mother."

I can't see either of their faces, but it feels to me like the silence gets even stonier.

The driver cracks first. "Just because you're gay?" He sounds puzzled. "There must be some other reason."

I know, I think. *Homophobia never makes any sense once you stop and think about it for half a freaking second.*

"Shut up," Curly says. "Just shut up. We're almost there."

I am out of ideas. And he's right. I feel the van pull off the main road, and before long we're easing into a garage. The automatic door shuts behind us as we come to a stop.

The driver yanks me out of the back while Curly keeps his distance, his firearm ready. He isn't stupid.

They march me into the house, and a painful twist of nostalgia corkscrews through me as I smell the mix of furniture varnish and leather and ash that is this house's scent. I never really noticed it before, but it brings back memories of a hundred other times I walked this hallway from the garage to Aiden's office. If the boxes full of wreaths and garland along the corridor are any indication, Aiden's domestic help are in the midst of putting up Christmas decorations, but I hear no voices, no sound at all. I suppose if you're going to kill a man, you send the help home early.

I'm startled that my handlers steer me up the stairs to the private parts of the house instead of to Aiden's study. The grand staircase is thickly carpeted, making our footfalls almost silent. It's slow going with my sore ankle, but they keep me moving. They bring me into a bedroom with barred windows. Bars to keep thieves out? Or the inhabitants of the house in?

Curly pushes me into the en-suite bathroom, unbinds my hands, and steps back to raise his weapon again. "Boots off. Pants off. There's a toilet. Use it. When we kick the shit out of you, we don't want it to be literal. Mr. Milford's carpets are new."

That almost makes me laugh. Aiden wants to hurt me, but he's worried about getting blood and shit on the carpet. If I rush them now, they'll shoot me . . .

But I don't want to be shot. I do as ordered, shedding what I'm wearing from the waist down and taking care of business.

Driver comes to the door with a cell phone to his ear. "Understood," he tells the caller, and hangs up. "Strip all the way," he says over Curly's shoulder at me.

I tamp down a prickle of nerves. They don't need me naked to kill me. A naked body's harder to hide than a clothed one. This doesn't bode well either way.

As I pull my shirt off, Curly asks, "Were you really Team Four?"

"I was. And my dad before me," I add for good measure.

"Come on," Driver says to us both. Out in the bedroom, he has set a metal folding chair on a half-folded tarp. "Sit."

The metal is cold against my bare ass. He binds my ankles to the legs of the chair, the rope biting painfully into my bad ankle, forcing my knees apart. Then he ropes my forearms together behind me and secures them to the back of the chair. How ironic to have spent weeks in the wilds of Maine in winter and never to have shivered as much as I am right now with my balls against the metal chair. Goose bumps rise all over me.

Driver picks up his phone again. When he speaks, all he says is, "We're ready."

A minute or two later the knob turns on the bedroom door and in comes Aiden. He's in neatly pressed slacks and a russet-red V-necked sweater. He shuts the door behind him and looks at me, then at Curly. "I'd keep your gun on him if I were you."

Curly raises an eyebrow but doesn't say anything. His hand emerges from behind the flap of his long duster and he shows Aiden his firearm, his finger along the barrel, ready to slip to the trigger if needed. Aiden nods and returns his attention to me.

"Eric, Eric, Eric." He sighs heavily. "What are we going to do with you?" The question isn't rhetorical, as he goes on to ask the other two, "What can we do to him that won't leave visible marks?"

"Excuse me?" Driver asks.

"You know." Aiden looks distinctly uncomfortable, swaying slightly by the door, not because they're discussing violence but because he doesn't know what he's talking about. "Like in that movie. Soap in a sock, right?"

The three of us in the room who are ex-military suddenly understand what he means. Curly speaks. "If you're thinking of *Full Metal Jacket*, Mr. Milford, I have to say the idea that soap in a sock leaves no bruises is a Hollywood myth."

"When they say 'no visible marks,' they usually mean none on the face," Driver adds.

"Shit. I was hoping . . ." He trails off as he pulls a long black dress sock with something heavy inside it from his pocket. "Well, I suppose if he's going to bruise up, anyway, I may as well still use this."

I wonder what he sees as he steps gingerly toward me, almost sidestepping as if he's afraid of me. He *is* afraid of me. I'm naked and tied to a chair, and he's afraid of me. I look him right in the eye as he nears.

I can take this, I tell myself. It's what I told myself all through BUD/S, all through hazing, all through everything Garrett and Ruiz and Cass put me through. *I can take this.*

Aiden swings the sock like David getting ready to fling a rock at Goliath and then whacks me right in the chest. He dances backward on the balls of his feet like he thinks he's Muhammad Ali now and like I might have a counterpunch despite my arms being tied. I breathe through my nose. He's never beaten a man before. That much is obvious.

He comes forward again, still bouncing on his feet like a cardio kickboxer. *Wham.* This time the bar of soap gets me in the stomach and I grunt a little. The only way to take this is to tense at the moment of impact. If he knew anything about working a guy over, he'd blindfold me so I wouldn't be able to tell when the blow was coming.

He's emboldened by each strike, though, and he starts hitting me harder and faster, giving me less time between wallops. I start to sweat with the effort of keeping myself together, of meeting each hit with tensed muscles. I can smell the fucking soap now, too. Ivory.

And then he gets me in the face, right on the temple, which snaps my head to the side. That rings my bell more than the impact of the soap itself. I blink as the sudden vertigo makes my mouth and eyes water.

Aiden's voice sounds like it's echoing through a coffee can. "Aww, look, I made him cry."

I strain against the ropes without even realizing that's what I'm doing, and Aiden backs up suddenly. If I weren't tied down I'd have my hands around his throat right now, and he knows it. I hear the *click* of a hammer being drawn, but my tunnel vision shows me nothing but Aiden's face as he struggles to put on an expression of fake bravado.

There's no way to win this war, but I feel I've won a battle.

"Keep an eye on him," Aiden says. He exits a bit more quickly than bravado should allow.

The door shuts. I catch Driver's eye roll before he schools it off his face. A minute later he checks the hallway, then says to Curly, "I'll get us some chairs."

Curly merely nods and takes up a stance with his firearm beside the door.

I let myself breathe again. I'm going to need my strength if it's going to get worse from here, and I'm certain it will.

Assess. Doesn't feel like any ribs broke. I can see the bruises coming up on my chest, though. It's sheer luck he didn't tag me in the solar plexus. Or in the eye. I still feel a little dizzy from the blow to the head, but it's not like I'm going anywhere.

Driver comes back. Curly takes a chair from him. "How about this. I'll take first shift. Who knows how long Milford's going to be at this?"

"At least until morning," Driver says. "I'll be in the kitchen making a sandwich."

I wonder what's meant to happen to me in the morning.

Curly positions the chair between me and the door and sits.

"So which branch of the service was he in?" I ask.

He doesn't move a muscle, not even a twitch, at first. But then he comes to some kind of decision. "Army Reserve," he says with no inflection in his voice whatsoever.

I just nod and then we sit together in silence.

FIFTEEN

Time stamp:
0004 Saturday, Milford Mansion, Duxbury, Massachusetts

I t's shortly after midnight. I know because the grandfather clock at the bottom of the stairs just rang. Curly leaves and Driver takes up his post at the door as Aiden prepares himself for round two.

This time he marches up to me—well, until he's a few feet from me—and takes his belt off. He doubles it over and slaps it against his palm. I hold in a sigh. Awakening Aiden's inner sadist wasn't on my wish list.

"I've always wanted to do this," he says, running the belt through his grip with a sick smile. "I never beat my son, you know that? Thought it was barbaric and might make him turn out twisted. That what made you a cocksucking son of a bitch, Eric? Did your daddy pull your pants down and spank your fanny?"

I should tune out everything he says, but somehow I can't. Instead, I try to concentrate on thinking, *I can take it.* I try to make it my mantra. *I can take it. I can take it.*

"No one'll question if you've got welts on your kinky, perverted ass," he goes on. "Not if what I saw in that file was true."

Although the leather belt is slightly less of a danger than the sock-soap flying hammer, it hurts like a motherfucker. Which is the point, I guess. Because of how I'm attached to the chair, he can only get at the upper part of my back and shoulders, and it isn't long before he returns his attention to my chest.

And then he starts working my inner thighs. He has to come close for this, and when he grabs me by the hair, I know we've crossed a line. He whips me furiously on the leg, catching my cock and balls sometimes, too. He's lost control, and I know in that moment that he'd kill me if he knew how. The only thing keeping me from screaming is that my jaw is locked shut.

And the only thing that saves me from even more pain and damage is that Aiden's out of shape. His arm gets tired. He's out of breath. He throws the belt on the floor and retreats to Driver's side, huffing and puffing like the big, bad wolf.

I've made it through another round.

Driver checks his watch and then the two of them go out into the hallway.

When Driver comes back in alone, he plants his butt in the chair. He lights a cigarette and sits there, glancing at me from time to time, but most of his attention is on smoking. I don't attempt to engage. I'm trying to recover, to get my mental armor back into place. I'm not afraid of Aiden killing me in cold blood, I realize. I'm afraid of him doing it by accident. If he put a gun to my head and said, "Hasta la vista, baby," I could make peace with that. But him losing it in a rage and choking me to death or putting an eye out—for some reason that idea gets under my skin.

I decide to engage after all. "Hey, how long's he planning to keep me like this?"

Driver looks me over and then walks close. He leans close until we can see eye to eye, and then he crushes out his cigarette right on the scar the bullet left on my shoulder. "You broke his boy. Now Milford wants to break you."

I stare at the floor and say nothing.

"Kid won't stop crying."

My head jerks up. *Chase is here?*

"Once Aiden's had his fill of you, he's handing you over. But don't get any funny ideas." He brushes the ash off my shoulder with monstrous gentleness. "If it was my own son, you probably wouldn't still be breathing. Make one wrong move and I won't hesitate to drop you."

He takes my silence as assent and goes back to ignoring me. I shut my eyes, trying to calm the maelstrom his words have stirred up in my head. They're going to hand me over to the police, which is good for my long-term survival prospects, but I barely care about my own survival or escape. What about Chase? The thought that he's here, broken and trapped, breaks my fucking heart.

SIXTEEN

Time stamp:
0600 Saturday, Milford Mansion, Duxbury, Massachusetts

I jerk awake for the millionth time, imagining that I can hear Chase crying. It's my imagination—or my conscience—torturing me, and it's a much worse torment than anything Aiden and his goons can come up with. I'm trying to conserve my strength for that, but every time my eyes close, there's Chase.

I should have just told you, I imagine myself telling him. *I should have tied you up and then just told you, "Look, your old man owes me. Nothing personal. I won't hurt you."*

The lump in my throat doubles when I remember that was exactly how it was supposed to go. I hadn't planned on fucking him, much less falling for him. This is one hundred percent my fault for not sticking to my plan. For giving in to my basest instincts. I deserve every shred of heartbreak.

But Chase doesn't.

I don't believe in God, but I pray anyway. *Dear God, if there's some way I can ever make it up to Chase, please let me. Let me make it right. That's all I've ever wanted to do: balance the scales of justice. I'll accept every punishment you throw at me if only it can be made right.*

The light of dawn is in the windows when Aiden returns for round three. He's in a bathrobe this time, and I can see his bare, hairy legs between the bottom of the robe and his shearling slippers. I swallow. That can't be good.

Curly is back, too, and they're in the middle of some kind of argument. About me? He cuts off as they enter the room, so the only words I hear are "—the most secure position."

Aiden comes all the way to me this time and grabs me by the hair. "No way am I taking any chances with this motherfucker. He can stay tied like he is."

"All right—" Curly starts to say and then stops as he realizes what Aiden is doing, which is fumbling with the knot of his robe belt with his free hand.

As Aiden's cock springs into the air near my face, Curly turns quickly away. He clearly really didn't want to see his boss's penis. He really didn't. Driver is somewhere at the periphery of the room, and I wonder if he's averting his eyes, too.

Aiden's shaft is thick, topped with a head that seems small in comparison. I feel the heat coming from it as if his outrage is stored in his dick.

He's jammed it into my mouth before I can grab a breath. Fuck. With one hand firmly gripping my hair and the other pinching my nose shut, he chokes me on his cock. There's no air for me anywhere and every muscle in my body tries to struggle, but there's nowhere to go. My vision's starting to go purple and black when he pulls back an inch, just enough for me to suck in a lungful before he plugs my throat again.

Fuck fuck fuck fuck. There's no time to think, no time to do anything but react as every cell in my body screams for oxygen. I always thought if I was forced into a situation like this, I'd bite down, I'd do all the damage I could, but that thought can't even make it through the desperation to breathe. He backs out only enough to give me a sip of air from time to time and then goes back to forcing me to deep-throat.

It's okay. It's just another of those tests where survival equals winning. In BUD/S you tread water while wearing boots and full uniform. An instructor forces your head under the water. Repeatedly. They make you lie on the beach with your head toward the water while the tide comes in. They spray you with fire hoses until you can't move, can't tell up from down. They force you into the surf, make you crawl across the beach and then back into freezing-cold water again and again.

It isn't the men who are most physically strong who make it through Hell Week. It's the ones who are mentally tough. As every muscle aches for oxygen, my backbrain locks onto the realization that I am tougher than Aiden. His strong front hides the weakest man I've ever known. And nothing, not even his cock down my throat, will ever change that. At that moment, I know all I have to do is wait him out.

The son of a bitch starts moaning like choking me on his cock is the most incredible sensation he's ever felt, like I'm the most talented whore in the world. He keeps me under for longer and longer until I actually black out, and then he wakes me up by smacking me in the face, a note of panic in his voice. "Open your eyes, cocksucker!"

It's an improvement when he grabs me by the hair with both hands and fucks my mouth for all he's worth. At least then I get partial breaths between the gagging and the snot.

His come burns so badly that I retch. But at least he's out of my mouth now. He smacks me hard across the face and I retch again, spitting up bile and come, but it's over.

It's over.

It takes a supreme effort of will to force myself to look up at him. All I want to do is hang my head and breathe. But I have to show him I'm not beaten. Even if it might be advantageous to pretend I am, I simply can't. I look up, spit deliberately, and then lick my ravaged lips.

The look of horror in his eyes as he backpedals a few steps is worth it.

"Was it good for you, Aiden?" My voice is rougher than two-day stubble. "Best come of your life, wasn't it? I feel sorry for all the whores you're going to choke on your dick just trying to get close to—"

His fist meets my face and makes me laugh and laugh and laugh as he flees into the bathroom. I've forced my enemy to retreat. I've won.

We can all hear Aiden vomiting. Driver shakes his head and leaves the room.

Curly comes closer, then dabs at my lip with a handkerchief. I hadn't even realized I was bleeding. Must be from when Aiden hit me right before he turned tail.

"Thanks," I say.

"Your first time getting waterboarded on a dick?" he asks casually.

"No," I answer. It's even the truth. First time with someone who wanted to kill me, though, so there's that. "Hey. Is Chase okay? I'm worried about him."

Curly pauses before deciding to answer me. "He's a tough kid. Tougher than his dad knows." He looks me over. "Even tougher since he came back from that island."

That doesn't jibe with what Driver said, about Chase crying all the time. Either one of them is lying, or Chase has been showing different faces to them. Which one is closer to him? "Were you the one who drove him to culinary school?"

"Yeah."

I can hear the water running in the bathroom now. Any second Aiden is probably going to emerge. "Promise me you'll take care of him," I say hurriedly. "He doesn't deserve any of this."

Curly chucks me under the chin with a knuckle as the bathroom door opens. "Shoulda thought of that before you kidnapped him," he says.

Aiden is green around the gills. He can't even look in my direction. He leaves without saying a word.

SEVENTEEN

Time stamp: Unknown. Midday Saturday, Milford Mansion, Duxbury, Massachusetts

I wake with a jolt, surprised to find I'm still tied to the chair. How I managed to fall asleep and stay asleep for a few hours, I have no idea. While in the service, I learned to grab some shut-eye in pretty odd situations. During Hell Week I fell asleep while paddling a boat and woke up when my face hit the back of the guy in front of me. But this is beyond that.

I roll my shoulders as best I can, bound the way I am, and flex my fingers. They tingle a little but not enough to worry about. My shoulders are going to hurt like hell when they untie me, though—the shredded one especially.

If they untie me. If I'm going to be transferred to police custody, it obviously hasn't happened yet. Are they waiting until Monday?

Driver is sitting across from me, looking tired and bored. My guess is he hasn't gotten a lot of sleep since they nabbed me either.

I should probably keep my mouth shut, but that bored look has an edge of hostility in it that I can't ignore. "You waiting to take your turn?"

He snorts and doesn't meet my eye. "I don't know what you're talking about," he says with a sarcastic lilt. "Did something happen to you while I was out?"

I fall silent, considering. Was all that tough talk from him before just talk? Or is he saying that if I blab to the police, he'll play dumb on the witness stand? He gets up and moves to the window, and it looks

CECILIA TAN

to me like he wants nothing more than to get the hell out of here. If I had to guess, I'd say he's more concerned about covering his own ass than Aiden's at this point.

I'm about to ask him if Aiden's made him any promises when he's summoned into the hallway for a confab.

When the door opens again, he returns, followed by Aiden and Curly. Aiden is in a pin-striped business suit minus tie. "Payback time," he announces.

As if it hasn't been already? I wonder, and then I realize the door is still open.

In comes Chase. He's in an off-white button-down shirt, cuffs so perfect it must be tailored, with sharp-creased slacks the color of cinnamon. His hair looks dark, slicked back, and he's wearing a fancy gold watch. He looks every inch the young-billionaire-in-training, especially his shark-lidded eyes. It's such a transformation that I wonder if this is what Curly meant when he said Chase was tougher since coming back from the island.

"Here he is," Aiden says to his son. "Your big, bad wolf. Just a pathetic pervert, ready to be sent to the rape factory known as private prison."

"Dad, honestly," Chase says with a huff. "Your fixation on anal rape isn't healthy."

Aiden laughs a little too heartily. "Just telling it like it is, my boy. You're, ahem, you're sure he didn't—?"

"No, for the last time, no." Chase steps up to me and folds his arms. "He did a lot of sick things to me, but he didn't rape me."

I wonder why Chase is lying about that.

"When I saw that photo, I assumed the worst," Aiden said, his voice softening.

Chase looks at his father, his stare stony. "I thought 'the worst' would have been me dead, no?"

"Of course, of course. You know what I mean." Aiden comes forward and puts his hand on Chase's shoulder. "You know I love you."

"Give me some room." Chase shrugs Aiden's hand away and then takes his watch off.

He lays it on the dresser nearby as Aiden backs up a step. "All right, I—"

Aiden doesn't get to finish what he says, or maybe I just don't hear it as Chase smacks me hard across the face, a stinging slap that makes my eyes water instantly and my ears ring. I'm still blinking and processing that he hit me when he slaps me across the other side—his left just as strong as his right. Wow. I feel strangely proud of him.

"Attaboy!" Aiden is saying. Apparently, he approves of this display of manhood from his progeny, too. "This is better than seeing a shrink, eh?"

I want him to hit me again. I deserve this, and worse, for lying to him and everything else. I wish Chase would tell the rest of them to leave so I could confess that. He obviously doesn't want them to know we had sex, so I don't want to give it away. But I want to say I'm sorry.

Chase grabs me by the chin and makes sure I'm looking into his eyes when he says, "I'm not afraid of you. *Do you hear me?*"

Do I? There's a look in his eye, an edge in his voice . . . Is he trying to tell me something or is he just venting? I don't think I'm imagining it. It feels like he's trying to tell me something. Is this all about him getting over being victimized, or is something more going on here? I prayed to be able to make things right, but I didn't dare pray for what I really wish for: Chase, mine again, whole and dear. Maybe the blows to the head have made me delusional.

"Do you think you deserve this?" he says.

I assume he means do I deserve his censure. I nod. "I promised I wouldn't hurt you. In that I failed."

His eyes narrow and he nods in return. Are we really understanding each other? Or is it just the intensity of my need to connect to him that makes me imagine it's there?

Curly touches his earpiece and clears his throat. "Gentlemen, Grandame Milford is approaching the front door."

"Chase, remember what we talked about," Aiden warns. "Your grandmother's here for a nice lunch. She isn't to know about any of this."

Chase lets go of me and looks down into my face. "This isn't over," he growls. "I'll be back."

His eyes flick toward the watch on the dresser. I'm the only one who can see his face. He turns on his heel then and marches out, the others following him, leaving me with Driver again.

He sits down and takes out his phone. From the motion of his thumb, my guess is he's playing solitaire.

Good. I need time to process what just happened. Chase's watch is still sitting on the dresser. That eye-flick. Did I imagine it? I'm sure I didn't. He knows the watch is there. He left it on purpose. *Watch . . . point?* Gooseflesh races across my shoulders as the realization hits me. It's a message. It has to be.

He left it on its side, angled toward me. I stare at the face for a few minutes before I realize the watch isn't running. It's a Breitling navigator-style watch that shows military twenty-four-hour time. It's set to 2010. What's going to happen at 2010?

I play back his words to me. *I'm not afraid of you. This isn't over. I'll be back.*

My heart starts beating harder than it did when Aiden was choking me. Can it be true? Can Chase be coming for me? If I can just hang on until 8:10 p.m.?

EIGHTEEN

Time stamp: Approximately 1600 Saturday, Milford Mansion, Duxbury, Massachusetts

The sun is setting and my bladder's blissfully empty. I convinced Driver that it was worth his while to help me piss into the Arizona Iced Tea bottle he'd just finished. It was that or let me piss all over myself and possibly everything in the room. He managed to do it without touching my dick with anything but the bottle. Keeping from getting gay cooties, I guess.

I hear voices and music from downstairs. A Christmas party. Got to keep up appearances, right? I wonder what they would do if I started screaming. Call the police? That won't help me much. Four hours until the time Chase's watch indicates.

I've been doing the math. Driver and Curly have been swapping off at regular intervals. If they keep up the pattern, it'll be Curly at the appointed time.

Something else must be set to happen at the top of the hour. If this were a military operation, I'd say that's when the diversion would be.

For the next four hours, I come close to going out of my skull, though. What if I'm wrong? What if Chase doesn't want me after all? What if he just wants to kick me in the nuts and hand me over? Will I get a chance to tell him I love him? Even letting the word "love" rip through my mind sends my adrenaline spiking and a cold sweat springing up on my skin. I need to be calm for whatever's going to happen. Calm and collected.

To keep my brain busy I go over the details of my fire team's former operations. Assess, plan, replan, execute. One of our deployments involved a ship that had been laying mines in the Persian Gulf. It looked like a freighter, but it was no innocent cargo ship. Unlike some, this operation involved every aspect of SEAL training, including diving and underwater demolition. It sounds like a simple plan—blow big holes under the waterline and let the fucker sink—but what sounds simple requires thousands of decisions to plan and execute. How will the insertion take place once the target is acquired? How will stealth be maintained? What type of explosives? Where on the hull would they do the most damage? What contingencies are in place for meeting resistance? And so on. That operation was a success. Maybe that's why my mind settles on that one: a smooth execution, a perfect outcome.

Or maybe it's because it was the last big operation the four of us were part of before discharge.

I really wonder where those guys are now.

The last time I saw Cass was in Virginia, after the final word came down. Garrett and Ruiz had already left, getting out before the military could change their mind and charge us with something worse, I guess.

Cass was packing up his things at his hotel, placing paired socks neatly into a suitcase on the bed. He'd started letting his hair grow, glossy and feathery brown as a starling. He had a touch of Texas in how he spoke, not an all-out drawl but a soft-spoken way of clipping his vowels short. "Ain't nothing to do about it now."

"You could come stay at my place for a while," I said. "My mother's a great cook. We can catch Amtrak right from—"

"No offense, Eric." He didn't look up from his packing. "But the last thing I want to do is hang around in the city right now."

My mother lived in the suburbs, but that close to New York counted as "city" to Cass.

I sat on the edge of the bed. I'd been inseparable from the three of them for years. I was having trouble imagining what life was going to be like without them.

"Hey."

I looked up. Cassidy was standing still, examining me. "They could've thrown the book at us, you know. It could've been a lot worse."

I knew. The brass had threatened us with jail and dishonorable discharge. They had settled for slightly nicer ways of kicking us out, but so-called "honorable" discharges under Don't Ask, Don't Tell weren't the slightest bit honorable. I felt like my life was over.

"C'mere." He beckoned me into a hug. My breath grew suddenly short as I tried not to cry.

The next thing I knew we were devouring each other, the suitcase and socks knocked to the floor as we wrestled each other out of our clothes on the bed. Mouths and tongues met genitals and hindquarters. I came while he was eating my ass, and he deposited one last load between my cheeks—not inside me but on my tailbone. I wouldn't have cared if he'd put it in without a condom that time, but old habits die hard.

And then we were lying there, side by side, panting like we'd sprinted a fifty. "You could . . ." I tried again, "still come and stay for a couple of days. I mean, if you haven't figured out what's next."

He hugged me hard enough to crack my spine. "Eric. What's next is you go out and fall in love. Everything from now to then will just be a blur. You'll meet that guy—or girl, I don't judge—and everything else will go *poof* into the past."

He was telling me goodbye. I knew it but I didn't want to hear it. "Okay, but what do I do with myself until then?"

Cass heaved himself off the bed and dug around in his things. He flicked me a business card. "Call this guy. He can help you find work. Security, bodyguarding, that kind of thing."

I tucked the card into my wallet and gathered up my clothes. I got into the shower. When I came out, Cassidy was gone.

Six months later I was working for Aiden Milford.

Driver yawns and gets up to pace. When someone radios him, he doesn't bother to go into the hallway to talk. "Yeah, of course I'm upstairs. Can't exactly leave this goon alone."

He nods as he listens through his earpiece to whoever's talking to him. "I'm really not worrying about the party guests. If the senator shows up, he'll have his own security. The rest of them? CEOs and lobbyists and a couple of town aldermen. The biggest security risk in that crowd is some wife accidentally putting on someone else's mink. You've already screened the caterers, right?"

More nodding. Then, "Okay, fine. Have Rick give the carolers a once-over when they get here. They're due to arrive at 7:30, perform at eight."

So that's what's at 2000. Joy to the world.

Time stamp: 1900

Time for the changing of the guard. Curly comes in with an exasperated look on his face, carrying a shopping bag.

Driver chuckles. "What, are the aldermen's wives giving you guff?"

Curly shakes his head. "I hate rich people."

"What's in the bag?"

"Christmas gifts for my kids." Curly lets out a long-suffering sigh and sits down in the chair. "Keep an eye on Milford, will you?"

Driver puts his jacket on and buttons it. "Drinking too much punch again? Last year he was like a petulant four-year-old who didn't like his bedtime."

"Exactly," Curly says. "Keep him out of here especially. Aiden's pet cop is coming for this guy tomorrow, and then we can all forget this happened."

"Too right," Driver says and leaves. They're both clearly ready for this whole incident to be off their records.

Curly checks his watch and locks the bedroom door. He places the shopping bag in the bathroom, checks his firearm, and chambers a bullet. Then he gets a knife out.

He moves behind me. "I don't trust you," he says. "But I trust Chase, and this is what he wants."

The momentary idea that he might shoot me in the back of the head flashes through my mind, but there's no fear. "I'm okay with whatever Chase wants."

"Good. Here's how we're going to do this. I'm going to cut a rope or two and then step back. You're going to free yourself the rest of the way, go into the bathroom, and put the clothes in that bag on. You're going to keep the door open so I can see you, and if you even twitch aggressively, I'll just fucking shoot you. Clear?"

"Loud and clear," I answer. The focus that sharpens when an operation is underway is a blessing. My heart is in my throat, but I don't care. I feel the tension on my arms go slack. I work my wrists free and then for the first time in many, many hours, my elbows are in front of my body.

It takes everything I have not to scream as my shoulder tendons are forced to move. Especially the left. After a few moments, I'm able to move my right arm but not my left. I rub the left shoulder with my right palm, trying to get it to come back to life. The scar from the bullet feels like a lima bean under my skin, and I remember almost tearing this arm from the socket while I was trying to keep from submerging in the water on the island. I wiggle my fingers, but I can't raise my arm higher than my chest.

"We don't have a lot of time," Curly prompts.

"Working on it." I get my legs free and flex my good ankle. The bad one—well, we'll see. I stand up slowly, my weight on the good leg, and shuffle forward. I won't be running any sprints anytime soon, but I can at least make it to the bathroom.

"Wash your face," he barks as I flip on the light. "Try to look presentable."

I see why when I dig the clothes out of the bag. A tuxedo jacket and pants, white gloves—a caterer's uniform. The tighty-whities look familiar. Chase's? No, wait. I'm pretty sure they're mine, and they're not the ones I was wearing when I left the island. Chase must have taken them when he fled. There's a lump in my throat, but I can't think about that right now.

In the medicine cabinet, I find some medical tape. I tape my ankle to stabilize it as best I can and then slip the black dress sock on over it.

"If you really want me to be hard to recognize, I should shave off the goatee," I say.

"There a razor in there?" Curly asks from behind his gun.

"There is."

"Do it."

I shave my face for the first time in two years. I'm lucky not to have a black eye. My lips are a little swollen but not enough to attract attention. The tuxedo is a bit tricky to get on with one arm not working right, but the really hard part is the bow tie. Thank goodness it's a clip-on.

In the bottom of the bag are shoes. They fit.

"Comb your hair," Curly says, sounding every bit like a chief to an underling. I slick it back with some gel from the medicine cabinet. He snorts. "You look like you're on the way to a wedding."

"Better than a funeral," I say.

With the gun, he motions me toward the watch on the dresser. Next to it is a folded piece of paper. I unfold it.

There's a map of the mansion and grounds. Chase's handwriting is achingly familiar. He's marked coordinates for me. A rendezvous point.

"You'll go at twenty-hundred," Curly says.

I put the watch on and wind it. "What time is it?"

He checks his own. "Four minutes till."

I adjust the time on the watch as he motions me to sit again.

I shake my head. I'm too nervous to sit. I go to the barred window instead, and he doesn't shoot me. I want to ask him what Chase plans to do at the rendezvous, but maybe he doesn't even know that. Instead I ask, "What's your name?"

"Briggs," he says, lowering the gun, but still holding it ready. He's not taking any chances on my sanity or my faith in the plan. I can't say I blame him.

A chorus of voices breaks into "Adeste Fideles," the sound coming right through the floor. "That is some group of carolers," I remark.

"About twenty of 'em," Briggs says and steps back further from me. "Time to mo—"

A triple knock comes on the door. He goes to it immediately, and I back against the wall where I can't be seen, just in case.

He opens the door for Chase, who rushes in, breathless, carrying an empty metal tray. He stares at me a moment—maybe shocked at my appearance—then lets the tray fall to the carpet as he grabs me by the face and kisses me.

When he lets me go, my mouth doesn't work. "You . . . That . . . I . . ."

Briggs says what I can't manage to. "I thought you were angry enough to kick him in the nuts."

"I was. I am," he says to me. "But I got a chance to slip away and had to come see you. The second I saw you . . ." He shrugs. "Let's get out of here."

I pick up the tray with my good arm. "What happens to Briggs when it turns out we're gone?"

Briggs snorts. "You think I'm planning to keep this job even one more day after this bullshit?"

Chase straightens my bow tie. "You sure?"

"I'm not afraid of your papa," Briggs says. "Don't you worry about me, Chay."

"All right." He turns to me. "Rendezvous on the far side of the mower shed."

I need to know more of the plan, though. "And from there?"

"Hoof it down to the convenience store and get an Uber, like always," Chase says.

Briggs curses under his breath. "This one's not hoofing it very far. Here." He pulls a car key from his pocket and hands it to me. "It's the Range Rover parked by the guardhouse at the bottom of the driveway. Ditch it when you can."

"Why are you giving the keys to me?" I ask, feeling like there are still things about this operation I don't know.

"Because Milford didn't want Chase to learn to drive," Briggs says. "Now, get going."

Chase does two more things before he goes into the hall. He slips my burner phone into my pocket. Just in case, I suppose. And he kisses my cheek. "See you at the shed."

He precedes me into the carpeted hallway and heads down the main staircase toward the festivities.

I head for the servant's staircase at the other end of the hall, holding the serving tray by one handle. I make it to the bottom of the stairs by taking gentle steps. My next goal is the kitchen, which has a back exit door. The kitchen is to the right from here, on the other side of the dining room. I wonder if the metal tray would stop a bullet if I had to use it as a shield?

It's better as camouflage. I can only hold the tray level when I tuck my bad arm against my ribs, but that looks all right. I'm carrying it down the hallway when two elderly men emerge from the parlor. Behind them I get a glimpse of the crowd of partygoers facing the Christmas tree at one end of the room, the carolers arrayed in front of it. The scents of spruce and candle wax send a sudden ache to have Chase in my arms all the way to the ends of my fingertips. One of the old men puts his empty champagne flute onto my tray and asks where the nearest restroom is. I indicate the hallway to one side, and then I duck into the dining room.

Nothing's changed in here since the day Aiden fired me—not the antique wood table large enough to seat twenty, not the glass chandeliers or the clinging scent of rancid cigarette smoke. I want to gag.

I push through to the kitchen, where a woman in chef whites grabs the tray and empty glass from me and hands me a full tray of canapés without even looking at me. She's already reaching for a whipped cream canister as she barks, "I don't care if they're still singing. Get out there before these get cold."

Back into the dining room I go, intending to set the tray on the table and slip out through the French doors. I can walk around to the mower shed from there.

The singing trails off suddenly as furious voices come from the direction of the foyer— Chase and Aiden flinging words at each other. Adrenaline surges through my veins, and I barely feel my feet as I leave the tray and rush toward the foyer. I hunker behind the archway while I assess the situation.

"No appreciation!" Aiden growls drunkenly. "No appreciation for anything I've done for you! Ungrateful!"

Chase is backing away from him, and Aiden follows him right into my line of sight as the full assembly of partygoers turns to watch the new spectacle. "Done for me?" His voice wavers with emotion, like he barely has enough air to speak, but he's determined to get the words out anyway. "You mean like lock me up here in the house like a prisoner?"

Aiden's voice is a blast from a volcano blowing its top. "Where do you need to go? You have everything you need right here! You're still a child!"

Chase is shaking but indignant. "I'm twenty-two years old!"

"You've got no education!"

"Because you wouldn't let me!"

"You never would've survived college," Aiden insists matter-of-factly. "You couldn't even make it through fourth grade."

Chase's shoulders fall back as he clears his throat and stands tall. His voice gains strength as he says, "Maybe if you'd given me a chance to mourn my mother instead of erasing her from our lives, I might have."

Aiden's red face goes pale. "You dare."

Chase sees me, his gaze locking on mine. "I do. I'm not the weakling I used to be, Dad. Not anymore."

A white-haired woman with more diamonds than an engagement-shop window pushes her way out of the staring crowd. "Aiden, what is the meaning of this? You're intoxicated and embarrassing the family."

"Don't you start now, Mother," Aiden says. "You were happy when I made the rule prohibiting the mention of certain people."

Chase seizes her hand suddenly. "Grandame. There's something I have to tell you."

"What is it, child?"

"Dad's gone nuts. He's telling people I was kidnapped when I went to Maine with my boyfriend."

I hear sharp gasps from various people in the crowd. Chase keeps hold of his grandmother's hand and pulls her in my direction. He's holding out his other hand. Toward me.

I step into the foyer to grasp his fingers.

"This is Eric," he says. "Eric, this is my grandmother."

I don't dare look at Aiden. "Pleased to meet you, Mrs. Milford," I say.

"Milford-Harrison," she corrects icily. "I remarried. Chase, dear, you know I've never approved of Aiden's way of raising you. But are you sure?"

"Sure of what?"

"Are you truly attached to this boy? Or is he merely a convenient rebellion against your father's wishes? I won't sanction you playing with people's hearts." At that pronouncement she glares in Aiden's direction.

It's the *click* of the hammer being drawn back on a gun that makes me turn toward him at last. He's regained his color—well on the way to a full purple rage. The pistol pointed upward looks like a Ruger .38, small but easily lethal at this range. "I am the head of this family," he declares. "And you will do as I say."

"Put that thing away," Grandame Milford-Harrison scolds.

Aiden pulls the trigger—the shot sending a shower of glass chandelier bits down onto us—and the majority of the partygoers hit the deck, their hands over their ears, the grandame included.

Chase barely flinches. He still has my hand in his. "Put the gun down, Dad."

"You don't tell me what to do. Nobody tells me what to do," Aiden growls.

"Put the gun down now, and everyone will go home with a story about that one time Aiden Milford got drunk at his own Christmas party and shot a hole in the ceiling," Chase says. "Any other choice and you're going to jail, Dad."

Aiden aims the gun at Chase, and I put myself between them.

Aiden clucks his tongue. "You just made my decision for me, cocksucker," he says. "Say goodb—"

Briggs drops on him from the railing of the grand staircase, and the gun goes off.

NINETEEN

Time stamp:
2024 Saturday, Milford Mansion, Duxbury, Massachusetts

The first time I took a bullet, it felt like someone had hit me in the shoulder with a sledgehammer. That time I hadn't had a moment to think. It had been pure reaction. Aiden had been attending a healthcare summit in Europe. The story that later emerged was that the gunman's actual target was the executives of Novartis, but at the time all I knew was I saw a barrel pointed in the direction of the person I was supposed to protect. I went for the gun and my next thought was, *Where the fuck did that sledgehammer come from?*

There on that Zurich street, a few moments went by before my brain processed the fact that the ringing in my ears was from the gunshot, and the reason my arm wasn't working was a bullet and not Thor's hammer. I grabbed my shoulder, but it didn't register that the reason my shirt was wet was my own blood. The pain didn't start until a minute or two later.

This time isn't like that. The pain is instantaneous, a burning sensation at the back of my jaw, which is confusing as fuck since the gun was in front of me, not behind. My first concern is still for Chase, though. I keep him behind me with my arms while I scan to make sure another threat isn't about to appear. But Briggs has Aiden flattened, the weapon in control, and the cacophony of multiple people calling the police simultaneously on their cell phones bounces around in my ears.

I feel Chase gripping me tightly from behind. "Take it easy, Eric," he says.

I reach up to soothe the burning spot by my ear and realize I'm bleeding profusely. Chase is lowering me to the ground. I can hear someone sobbing.

It's not him. "First aid," he says, to himself, I think. "Stop the bleeding. That might be tricky." Then to me: "Keep your head forward. I don't want you to choke on the blood."

I nod in agreement. I think I know what's happened. The bullet entered through my mouth and exited somewhere in the vicinity of my ear. There are a lot of important arteries there, and you can't tourniquet your neck. I agree with his first-aid assessment. Tricky.

I'm bleeding from the mouth, but I'm breathing.

If I'm breathing, I'm alive.

If I'm alive, I can say what I've been meaning to. "Chase."

"Don't talk. Help is on the way." He's pressing a cloth against the exit wound on the side of my face while he keeps hold of me around the chest from behind.

I don't know if I'm going to get a chance to say this again. "Listen. I have to tell you something."

"You're sorry? You told me that already," he says through gritted teeth. My tough scout. "Apology accepted."

"No." I breathe in too quickly and cough from inhaling my own blood. Each cough makes everything in my body hurt—my ankle, my shoulder, my lungs, my mouth. But I feel bathed in warmth when I say, "I love you."

His embrace tightens. "I need you to stay quiet. I need you to live through this, Eric."

"I love you," I say again. I can't say much else without risking another coughing fit. My consciousness is starting to fade. It feels like I'm falling asleep, going limp in his arms, and for a moment I dream we're in the lean-to.

"Eric!"

I can't answer. I can only pat his hand on my chest with my own.

"If you want to hear me say it in return, you have to live—do you understand? You have to live through this. You have to. Can you hear me?"

We're in the lean-to. We're safe under the snow, and the racket is the storm outside, and my toes are a little cold but that's to be expected. I'm in his arms where I belong, and that's all that matters.

TWENTY

Time stamp: 0857 Sunday, Beth Israel Deaconess Hospital, Plymouth, Massachusetts

I can see the clock on the wall reads almost nine, but I don't know if that's a.m. or p.m., and I feel a small jolt of panic, wondering if Mom got her morning medicine like she was supposed to or . . .

The panic subsides as I realize I'm the one hospitalized. I'm strapped to a bed in a sitting position. My head is muzzy and my tongue feels furry and gross, but I can move it to feel something wadded inside my mouth.

Hey, I'm alive.

That's as much excitement as I can take and I drift back to sleep, post-surgery anesthesia still swirling around in my system.

The next time I open my eyes, I'm in a different room and I'm lying down. I can move my tongue more freely, and although I really want a drink of water, I decide life will be perfect if I can just move my hand enough to touch Chase on the hair. He's asleep in a chair next to me, his face and arms on the bed, one hand on my leg. It takes some doing to move that arm, and I wonder if I've got any tendons left in my shoulder at all.

My fingers land on the back of his neck, and he purrs but doesn't wake up right away. When he does, he sits up suddenly and blinks.

He grasps my hand. "I was having a dream we were at the cabin."

I nod, not sure if I can make my voice work or not. My whole throat is dry.

"Here. They left me some ice chips for when you wake up." He slips away from me, but only for a moment. His fingertips against my lips as he puts a piece of ice into my mouth are all I want.

The ice is good, too, though. I try his name first. "Chase."

"Eric." He lets himself smile, and the worry lines melt away. "You're going to be okay."

I reach up to touch the bandage on the side of my face.

"The bullet went right through your cheek. No major damage to your jaw. Pretty clean, they said." He appraises my face coolly. "I asked the doctor to check if you had any wisdom teeth, though. You're such a stupid motherfucker." Angry tears redden his eyes, and I squeeze his hand.

"I know. I know." My voice wears down to a rasp, and he brings me more ice. When my mouth loosens up, I try talking again. I can only really get words out the non-swollen side of my face. "I never meant to lie to you."

"Of course you didn't. You're so stuck on honesty and keeping your promises that you thought it made sense to send me back to my father." He looms over me, but it's hard to feel anything but gratitude that he's here and I'm alive to see him. My hand finds the controls for the bed, and I motorize myself into sitting upright.

Now I can look him in the eye. "I wouldn't have. I never would have forced you." I want to say a mouthful, but I can only get these short sentences out. "Once it sank in. If we'd had a chance to talk about it."

He puts one hand on my thigh, gripping my fingers with the other. "If you'd just let me cool off on my own, we would have."

"I was afraid you'd die. In the snow."

"And instead you almost died in the snow." He squeezes my fingers. "Do you remember anything about me rescuing you?"

I shake my head. "Only nightmares."

"You were delirious. I was afraid you were still going to die. I took the boat to the mainland and called Briggs. I didn't know who else to call."

"You handled the crick?" The Zodiac, I mean. Slipping into SEAL jargon. Proves I'm still a little out of it.

"You taught me well, Eric," he says, and he doesn't sound angry at all.

The wheels are turning in my head now, though, as I try to put all the pieces together. "How did you call Briggs? I'd locked your phone."

"There's a hack. You don't need to unlock the phone to ask Siri for the time, and when she brings up the clock, you can access the app store to buy more alarm tones, which makes the phone active. It usually only works for one phone call before Siri gets wise, but that was all I needed." Without warning, he plasters himself against me in a half hug. "God, I'm glad you're alive."

"I'm glad you're . . . so fucking smart." I've got one arm wrapped around him, and the pain I feel is entirely over the fact that I can't hug him properly.

"Yeah, well, if we'd both been a little smarter, maybe we'd still be on the island." He kisses me on the forehead and sits back. "Or on our way to somewhere easy, breezy, and tropical."

"We still could."

He looks me in the eye. "All my life I dreamed about running away. You know what I learned from all this, though? Starting when I ran out of the cabin?"

The lump in my throat has nothing to do with the bandage. "What?"

"I learned I can't run away from my problems. It just creates more problems." He's got circles under his eyes from lack of sleep, but he is gorgeous in his strength. "I had to find another way to win."

"Where's Aiden?"

"Rotting in jail until tomorrow. Super-high bail amount. Takes a while to raise that kind of cash. His liquid reserves are suspiciously low." Chase examines his fingernails nonchalantly, then places a finger on my lips as if to hush me. "We'll probably both need to take the stand against him if we're going to make sure he goes to jail for a long time. He'll no doubt resurrect that cockamamie story about you being a kidnapper."

He's so fucking smart. They won't be able to prove where the ransom money went, of course, given the anonymous nature of

Bitcoin transfers and my other precautions. No matter what Aiden says now, it'll appear he went to extremes to keep Chase and me apart.

Nonetheless. "I was his employee," I point out. "Suspicious."

"Which is how we met, of course," Chase replies. "Briggs will testify, too. My lawyer thinks the fact that Dad tried to shoot you in front of several dozen witnesses is going to overshadow most other points."

He might be right. I take his hand in mine again. "So. No more running away."

Chase stands up, leans over, and plants a cautious kiss on my lips. "I understand we have millions of reasons to skip the country. I'm a cook. I can get work anywhere."

I squeeze his hand hard. "But you want to fight."

"I do." His eyes are cool. "But you must have had somewhere you intended to go."

After collecting the ransom and handing him back to his father, he means. The truth is I put most of my planning into the abduction part of the operation, not my escape. Maybe part of me never expected it to succeed.

I certainly never expected this. "I won't go anywhere without you, now."

"You better not," Chase says. "Because I love you." He kisses me again, much harder than before, hard enough that I feel the bullet wound ache. It's the best ache in the world.

EPILOGUE

Time stamp: 1145, Wednesday, Pickerel Bay

I exit the boat headfirst, entering the water unencumbered by gear. The only thing weighing on me is the question of my shoulder. The summer sun is scorching, but the water this far north is bracingly cold, even in July. I settle into my stroke rhythm, feet kicking, and it feels good. After months of physical therapy in a chlorine pool, being in the ocean feels great, the waves rocking me as I make for the island. Five hundred yards. This is a five-hundred-yard swim.

The beach comes up before I know it, and I find myself running up the strip of sand, raising my arms in triumph—another thing I couldn't do for months after they reconstructed my shoulder.

Chase's whoop reaches my ears from across the water and he guns the engine, speeding the Zodiac toward me. When he's near, though, he turns about. "I want to try," he shouts.

"All right." I dash back into the water and into the boat. "Five hundred yards in the ocean feels different than in a pool, though."

"Which is why I want to try it," he says, leaning into the wind.

I use the laser range finder to determine when we're five hundred yards out again, in roughly the same patch of water as when I'd done it. We switch places and I take the tiller. "I'm going to trail you," I tell him. "Just in case." A shark could appear. He could get a cramp. Sometimes people panic for no real reason when they're in open water. I can't stop these thoughts from going through my head, but I can be ready to react if any of these things actually happen.

"Yes, sir," he says with a wink and dives off the Zodiac into the water. My heart starts to hammer as he takes a long time to come up, but when his head breaks the surface, he's much further away than I expect. I hadn't realized he'd become such a strong swimmer. I guess all that time hanging around in the pool while I was doing my rehab has paid off. He came with me to every session.

He made me remember what it's like when someone has your back. Maybe that's why I didn't just put my shoulder back together in rehab. I put my head back together.

I nudge the engine to pace him, a safe distance to one side. We're more than halfway there, but I can see he's slowing. He raises his head more often to see how far there is to go. He pauses to tread water.

"You didn't tell me there was a current," he shouts breathlessly.

"I told you the open ocean is different from a pool!" The movement of the tide can make it like a treadmill, lengthening the distance.

He takes a few deep breaths and then resumes his swim.

When he's within a hundred yards, I start shouting encouragement. He's so tired he can barely lift his arms and he's switched to a breaststroke, trying to time each stroke to match the rhythm of the waves, to go with the water instead of against it. He's the most beautiful thing alive.

"You're almost there, Chase. Come on, you can do it."

I can feel how much he wants it, how much he wants to reach that beach and feel that triumph. But he's exhausted. I want to leap into the water and help him, but there's no way to do that unless he really gets in trouble. My heart is banging as if I'm the one clawing my way across the surface of the sea. *Come on, Chase. You can do it. You gorgeous creature.*

The cliff of the island looms as we near the beach, and he raises his head, feeling the shift in the water as the waves start to roll. He strokes and strokes and strokes and suddenly catches one at the right moment, and it carries him forward and deposits him far up the firm-packed sand. He lies there, unmoving, like a gift from Poseidon.

I beach the Zodiac moments later, hastily loop a line around a scrub tree, and then run toward him. As I near, I see he's panting, smiling, but too exhausted to move his limbs. I find myself pressed against his wet skin, suckling the salty sensitive spots on the back of his neck and wanting him beyond all reason.

It's a simple thing to strip two Speedos and even simpler to bury my tongue between his cheeks, adding wet to wet. And then it isn't my tongue I'm burying, but my cock. At last he lets loose the triumphant cry I've been waiting to hear. This is everything I can imagine wanting. All the meticulous planning in the world could ensure food and shelter and water, the elements of survival, but there was no way to plan for the filling of the hole in my heart. The hole that was torn when my father died, enlarged when my team was blown apart (not by a bomb but by the Navy itself), and made a crater by my mother's passing. It takes a love the size of the ocean to fill it, and that's what we have.

That's what we have.

Explore more of our holiday stories for charity!
riptidepublishing.com/titles/collections/2017-
holiday-charity-bundle

Riptide's 2017 Charity Bundle

Benefiting The Russian LGBT Network

Featuring:
Roan Parrish
Katie Porter
Cecilia Tan

Dear Reader,

Thank you for reading Cecilia Tan's *Watch Point*!

We know your time is precious and you have many, many entertainment options, so it means a lot that you've chosen to spend your time reading. We really hope you enjoyed it.

We'd be honored if you'd consider posting a review—good or bad—on sites like **Amazon, Barnes & Noble, Kobo, Goodreads, Twitter, Facebook**, **Tumblr,** and your blog or website. We'd also be honored if you told your friends and family about this book. Word of mouth is a book's lifeblood!

For more information on upcoming releases, author interviews, blog tours, contests, giveaways, and more, please sign up for our weekly, spam-free newsletter and visit us around the web:

Newsletter: tinyurl.com/RiptideSignup
Twitter: twitter.com/RiptideBooks
Facebook: facebook.com/RiptidePublishing
Goodreads: tinyurl.com/RiptideOnGoodreads
Tumblr: riptidepublishing.tumblr.com

Thank you so much for Reading the Rainbow!

RiptidePublishing.com

ACKNOWLEDGMENTS

I have several people to thank for the existence of this book, some of whom I'm not even sure I remember. I blame the open bar. We were at a publishing party at the RWA National convention in San Diego, on a rooftop deck overlooking the water. The waitstaff had been plying us with some kind of strong cocktail all night. This party also had enough chocolate-covered strawberries to fill the hold of a battleship. Several romance writers including Elizabeth Hoyt, Rebecca Zanetti, and a few of the publisher's staff were making a valiant attempt at eating as many as we could. (Or maybe that was just me doing that . . .) At any rate, the evening was glorious, and the conversation turned to the romance genre. Someone asked, Hey, what's the hot thing these days? And one piped up with Navy SEALs. Navy SEALs are the hottest thing right now. (In San Diego especially.) Billionaires, said someone else. Billionaires are still dominating the market. (Pun intended.) A third chimed in with, Abductions. Abduction and dark romance is the new hot thing. And I jokingly said, Oh yeah? I could write a romance where a Navy SEAL abducts a billionaire. Or maybe his hot son . . . And Elizabeth Hoyt seized my arm and said, Oooh, I'd read that.

I woke up the next morning two hours before my alarm with the entire book plotted out in my head. Eric started talking to me right away and narrated the opening chapter almost exactly as you see it here. Funny how inspiration works, isn't it? So thank you, Elizabeth—you woke this sweet, angst-ridden SEAL in my head and inspired him to tell his story. And thank you to Sarah Lyons for being persistent with the invitation to Riptide's charity bundle, which undoubtedly kept my subconscious simmering. I love it when a plan comes together.

Thank you to my beta readers, Mark Treble, Lenalena, Priscilla Yuen, and Julie Cox. You helped Eric make sense to himself as well as the rest of the world.

Lastly, thank you to the Girl Scouts of the United States of America. Eric's wilderness camping experience is lifted wholesale from "Survival Weekend" at Camp Hoover with my troop. First badge I ever earned was the camping badge, and all that stuff about birch bark and building lean-tos is completely true.

ALSO BY
CECILIA TAN

ABOUT THE AUTHOR

Cecilia Tan is the award-winning author of many passionate stories, including *Daron's Guitar Chronicles*, *The Prince's Boy*, and the Magic University series. In her life she has been a Girl Scout, martial arts instructor, professional skier, baseball writer, and sexuality activist, in addition to her fiction writing. (Eric's story about learning to light a fire with one match and build a lean-to is true.) On her shelf sits the National Leather Association's Lifetime Achievement Award for BDSM community activism, right next to the Romantic Times Career Achievement Award. She was inducted into the Saints & Sinners LGBT Writers Hall of Fame in 2010. She loves cats, travel, and cooking, as anyone knows who follows her on social media.

Join her mailing list at bit.ly/ctannews or follow her on the platform of your choice:
Website/blog: blog.ceciliatan.com
Medium: medium.com/@cecilia_tan
Facebook: facebook.com/thececiliatan
Twitter: twitter.com/ceciliatan
Instagram: instagram.com/ctan_writer
Tumblr: tumblr.com/blog/ceciliatan
Pinterest: pinterest.com/ctanwriter
Goodreads: goodreads.com/author/show/65430.Cecilia_Tan

Enjoy more holiday stories at RiptidePublishing.com and help a charity!

2016 Holiday Charity Bundle – The Trevor Project
riptidepublishing.com/titles/collections/2016-holiday-charity-bundle

Home for the Holidays – Ali Forney Center
riptidepublishing.com/titles/collections/home-holidays

Share the Love – It Gets Better Project
riptidepublishing.com/titles/collections/share-the-love

Love for the Holidays – Gay, Lesbian, Bisexual and Transgender (GLBT) National Help Center
riptidepublishing.com/titles/collections/love-for-the-holidays

Earn Bonus Bucks!
Earn 1 Bonus Buck for each dollar you spend. Find out how at RiptidePublishing.com/news/bonus-bucks.

Win Free Ebooks for a Year!
Pre-order coming soon titles directly through our site and you'll receive one entry into a drawing for a chance to win free books for a year! Get the details at RiptidePublishing.com/contests.

RIPTIDE PUBLISHING

www.ingramcontent.com/pod-product-compliance
Lightning Source LLC
Chambersburg PA
CBHW031237260626
47169CB00007B/2332